**Blood will be spilled & bonds will be tested...**

Ava's not afraid to get a little bloody... unless it comes to matters of the heart, that is.
When things get too close for comfort with Jake Dallas, Ava finds herself packing her bags to rescue a friend from the pitfalls of internet dating... with the vampire who bit her. What could go wrong?

Cassius knows the clock is ticking and he will have to make a choice—turn Ava into a monster like him, or feed on her blood until there's nothing left.
When Cassius discovers his corpse blood supplier has gone missing, he and Ava embark on a rescue mission that will test Cassius's loyalty in more ways than one.

Can Ava and Cassius work together to slay the monsters that lurk in the shadows as well as the ones in their hearts?

*Blood & Ash is book three in the Ava Crowley, Vampire Slayer series, filled with snarky heroines, sexy-as-sin monster hunters, and other seductive supernatural beasts.*

Blood & Ash

Ava Crowley, Vampire Slayer

Book Three

Copyright ©2023 Ariel Dawn


ISBN: 978-1-77357-511-7

978-1-77357-509-4

978-1-77357-510-0


Naughty Nights Press LLC

Cover Design by Willsin Rowe

# BLOOD & ASH

## AVA CROWLEY

## VAMPIRE SLAYER

## BOOK THREE

## ARIEL DAWN

NAUGHTY NIGHTS PRESS LLC • CANADA

These sudden joys have endings. They burn
up in victory like fire and gunpowder.

*— William Shakespeare*


What fire does not destroy, it hardens.

*— Oscar Wilde*

# CHAPTER ONE

"HARDER," AVA BREATHED as her back was slammed up against the wall. A sheen of sweat had already started to form on her skin, and her muscles were starting to ache, but she didn't care. Dallas grunted in response, his hand around her throat.

"Is that all you've got?" she said with a smirk. His fingers rested there, just above her jugular, and a part of her wanted to feel the force, the tight grip she knew he was capable of. Because in those moments, the ones that were far more frequent these days than they'd been before, she was free.

Free from the nightmares that plagued her, free from the ghosts that haunted her.

Well, the vampire who haunted her, really. Though with the way Cassius appeared and disappeared at will like the wind, he was quite ghostlike at times. Always there, watching.

Waiting.

Ava brought her lips to Dallas's, forcing the thoughts away. She could taste the saltiness of the sweat on his lip, the metallic taste of blood that hadn't quite dried yet from their last go-around in the ring, or more accurately, the mattress of Motel 6 that was acting as a boxing ring in place of the Bat Cave's comfortable gym.

"You drive me up a fucking wall, you know that?" Dallas bit back as he moved his lips from hers to her neck. Ava started to feel lightheaded from all of it—the sparring, the secrecy, the memories, the feel of Dallas and all his hardened edges encompassing her.

Now was her chance. She wrapped her legs around his waist, dragging her nails up his arm, fingers finding their way into his hair, twisting softly before tightening her grip.

She forcibly yanked his head to the side.

"Oh I know, Dallas, that's the fun of it," she said between breaths.

Dallas smiled devilishly back at her

before breaking her tight hold, his eyes full of heat and desire.

Desire that echoed beneath her skin.

Her muscles ached, her head was splitting, and she was certain she'd be sore tomorrow, but she didn't care.

It was getting harder and harder to care, and a part of her almost *wished* the others would knock on the door, would find them tangled up together so that she could breathe again. She hated lying to her brother, hated having to pretend everything was fine and nothing had changed, when in fact, *everything* had changed.

Dallas slid his hands underneath her thighs, turning her around before slamming her back onto the mattress of messy sheets once more, his weight heavy on top of her.

Ava wriggled and writhed beneath him as his large hand held her wrists together, his grip firm. She moved around, twisting and turning, her breasts brushing against his sweat-soaked chest. In the amber light of the motel room, he looked like every dream, every fantasy, every bad decision a girl could ever dream of.

"Fight me, Ava," he growled, grinding his rigid length against her thigh.

She grunted and huffed in annoyance, her muscles tightening, her leg starting to go numb from the weight.

It wasn't all that different from the first time they'd done this, four years ago. She could still remember how it felt when he wrapped his arms around her, held her close. How badly she'd wanted to submit and give into the temptation of

Jake Dallas, even then.

But now...

"Jake," she whined, a strange feeling working its way up her body, through her blood, into her heart, her mind.

"I can't, I—" Her breath started to come in faster, and panic started to set in.

She was trapped, and there was no way out.

"Fight me, Kitten. I know you can," he said, his voice strained, but yet full of something she'd never heard before.

"I don't want to fight!" she bit back, tears starting to form behind her eyes.

Dallas loosened his grip but he did not let go. Instead, he entwined his fingers with hers in a soft gesture that felt foreign to her. Jake Dallas wasn't *soft* in any sense of the word. No, Dallas was a force of nature, a hurricane that would undoubtedly wreck her and destroy her into a million pieces.

But still, she wanted the wrath of his storm. She wanted to be caught up in the eye of all that he was, because death was not an option. As long as she wore Cassius's mark, death would one day come for her and she would not submit to it. Not over her dead body.

"Ava," Dallas's voice turned softer, his free hand pushing her sweaty, wet strands of hair behind her ear. When she looked up into his eyes, she could see her own fear reflected in them, and she hated it. She hated herself for not being strong enough.

"Ava, I—" He brushed his thumb over her bottom lip.

Her heart racing, the world around

her started to fade back into reality, and she swallowed harshly.

"I can't do this right now," she said as she fought the tears.

Dallas was quiet for a moment, his gaze settling on her. He let go of her wrists, easing his weight off of her. She expected him to just leave her alone. That was what he normally did when she'd been pushed too far; given her space to ground herself again. Training with Dallas was always like that; it always pushed her past her limits, because the intent was to be stronger than her fears. To be strong enough to survive vampire Jedi-mind tricks as well as to combat their strength. It was the difference between life and death, and it was familiar.

But the tears weren't.

"I don't know what happened, I just—"

Dallas wrapped his arms around her and pulled her into his lap, brushing his fingers along her arm in the gentlest of touches. He tilted her head up, and looked in her eyes in a way that was quite different than the other times. The heat, the lust had diminished and in its place was something far more dangerous.

Sympathy.

The touch felt... intimate.

Loving almost.

"Don't look at me like that," she said as she pushed him in the chest, though not hard enough to move him, though she could have. If she wanted.

"Like what?" he asked, his brows furrowing in concern.

Ava didn't like it.

"Like I'm some fucking damsel in distress. I don't need your pity, I just... need a fucking break." She shoved him, and he fell back against the mattress, running his hand over his face.

"From this—" He motioned to the hotel room, which looked to be in disarray from their steamy 'sparring' session. "—or..."

The words hit Ava like a brick as she considered them. She moved off the bed, snatching up her clothes from the floor that had come off at some point after the second round, when sweat and heat made them both uncomfortable.

Ava froze.

Before she could even speak, both of their phones started going off, rattling against the end table. Dallas sighed, getting up from the bed as she pulled on her Blue Oyster Cult shirt.

"It's Mal," Dallas said, turning to her.

"Yeah, and?" She slid her jeans on slowly.

"Get your stake. We have a nest to infiltrate." He said the words plainly, as if they were the most normal thing in the world. As if the strange moment they'd just shared, the one where he *held* her hadn't happened at all.

*Maybe it's better if I just try and forget about it. Forget about today, forget about whatever this is that's happening between us.*

Ava nodded as she buttoned her jeans.

"Riding separately?" she asked, her nerves starting to settle.

Dallas stood there, the light of his phone illuminating him and his double star tattoos, the shadows falling on the planes of his chiseled jaw, his dark features.

He nodded. "Of course."

"All right. See you there," she said as she grabbed her phone, silencing it and sliding it into her pocket before throwing on her leather jacket. She reached for the door, pausing for a moment.

It was just a moment, a split second of waiting as she realized Jake Dallas did nothing to stop her. He did not protest or beg her to stay. Instead, he let her walk out the door and into the crimson sunset without a sound.

Ava settled into her Impala, turning the keys in the ignition.

The familiar guitar strings of *Heart's Magic Man* filled the car, and Ava sighed as she backed out of the Motel 6 parking lot, speeding off for the highway, off to hunt something she could catch.

# CHAPTER TWO

CASSIUS WATCHED THE rain fall outside the window. The days were getting shorter now, and fall, it seemed, had started to settle into Chester once more. The moon hung in the sky, lighting up the property he called home. The dark, black waters of the pool reflected the moonlight like a mirror, and the sight was almost soothing. Almost enough to get lost in.

The house was far too quiet for his liking, with Jasmine and Tajiri gone until daybreak. The silence never used to bother him as much as it seemed to these days. In fact, he'd enjoyed it once. His pulse thumped away beneath his skin faintly, his insides warming instinctively.

*She is near.*

He knew without a doubt, the stolen pulse in his veins belonged to the one and only Ava Crowley, the very reason for all his restlessness.

The desire to be near her, even in this moment, was damn near too much to bear as thunder roared in the distance.

Four years.

It had been *four years* since he'd tasted her blood on his tongue, since he'd marked her as his... mate.

Cassius watched the rain as it fell against the glass, long drops seeding into other drops until they connected and dispersed, the moonlight illuminating them like fractured diamonds.

When he could not stand the shadows of his own loneliness anymore, he grabbed his leather coat—a proper coat that came down well past his hips and near to his ankles—and slipped on his boots. Perhaps a walk through a November rain would be just the thing to clear his head.

He slid his cell phone in his coat pocket, if only out of habit. It wasn't as if he made many calls on the thing, but Ava did have a tendency to text him once in a while.

*When she needs my help on a case...*

Cassius shut the door as he stepped outside into the woods, the scent of rain most invigorating to his senses. A rainstorm in Chester during the fall was nothing quite like a rainstorm at the beach in Italy, or a rainstorm in Paris, but it was not without its grandeur and romance. There was something about the stillness of the forest when it stormed that soothed Cassius's spirit.

His stomach growled, and he fought to ignore it. It was Saturday, after all, and Brian would not be working the weekend shift, which meant he would have to wait a few days for his routine serving of corpse blood.

Before he knew it, he'd made his way out of the forest and into town, a deep sigh escaping him as his pulse ebbed with intensity. He stood on the side of the street, underneath a bright streetlamp, scanning his surroundings. She was close, so very close he could almost taste her. The memory of her blood in his mouth on that fateful night, the night both of their lives had been forever changed, would always be burned in his brain. He'd only bitten her to start the healing process, to save her from death's doorstep.

His venom had sealed her wounds, but it appeared it had opened some new ones as well.

For ever since that night, Ava Crowley had made it more than clear where he stood with her; yet time and time again, it seemed the opportunities to end his life had passed them by without their noticing. It was hard for him to believe she truly wished him dead, but he was not certain she had accepted his presence for it what it truly was, either.

A mate bond.

A bond that meant he'd claimed her blood.

Claiming a mate was something he'd never intended, and he didn't wish to commit Ava to a life of immortality, no matter how bad he wanted her for the rest of his cursed existence. As an Aurelia—a pure bloodline among his kind—he possessed the ability to sire a mate, a feat that had become much more rare nowadays. Though, being born into a high coven bloodline, Cassius knew what it was like to not have a choice in such things, and he vowed not to take such a choice from the spitfire that was Ava Crowley.

Cassius leaned against the streetlight

post as the rain fell, a symphony around him. Puddles rippled with fresh raindrops, and water ran down the sides of the cracks of the road, diverging into sewers. He watched as the neon purple lights in the window of The Third Eye dimmed, as the bell atop the door jingled in tandem. But it was not Ava who exited the shop, and for a moment his heart sunk.

Had he dreamt it?

Fantasized such things?

The pulse beneath his skin was still hot, still aching...

"Looking for someone?" The venomous tone was music to his ears, and a smirk formed on his face at the sound. He did not turn around. There was no need. He'd know that bite anywhere.

"Not anyone in particular," he teased.

"You're a terrible liar, Cas, you know that, right?" Ava huffed, and he could practically hear her eyes rolling in the back of her head, and he finally turned around to look at her.

She was dressed in an oversized maroon hoodie and ripped jeans, her hands in the frayed front pouch. The hood covered her short, brown hair, but he could still see several strands peeking out the sides. She took a step closer, and he pretended not to notice.

"I have never lied to you, Ava. Nor do I have the need or desire to do so."

Ava rolled her eyes as he pushed off the streetlamp post, taking a step closer to her.

She crossed her arms.

"Then tell me the truth. Why are you

standing like a fucking stalker outside my place of work?" she said as she chewed her lip.

Cassius let out a soft chuckle.

"Would you believe me if I said I wanted to clear my head?"

"Well, I didn't think you had any brains underneath all those golden locks, so no. I do not believe you," she said as she narrowed her eyes at him.

"You are a terrible liar, my sweet Avarice," he said with a grin.

Somehow gravity had pulled them closer, close enough he could reach his hand out and push back her hood, run his fingers through her chocolate brown hair, kiss her perfectly pink lips, and watch the blood he'd claimed flush into her cheeks.

But all he could do was stand there

like a stone, captivated by the sight of the woman who made him feel less like a monster and more like a man.

"I have no reason to lie to you, *Cassius.*" She hissed as she said his full name, something she did not do very often, if at all.

The sound of his name on her tongue made his slow, dying heart spring to life.

# CHAPTER THREE

AVA'S HEART THUDDED in her chest as she realized she was close enough to kill Cassius without a second thought. It would be easy. She could slide her hand beneath her shirt—beneath Dallas's hoodie—and swiftly pull out her stake she kept tucked in the band of her bra.

With the way Cassius was looking at her, his gorgeous green eyes full of sparking embers, she could not look away. Surely he was doing *something* to her to make her stand so still. She knew without a doubt what a vampire's thrall felt like, and at this moment, she did not feel that. Perhaps it was some type of vampire juju that was special to this pain in the ass vampire who filled her thoughts more than she wished to admit.

Ava could feel her blood heat, rushing through her veins. In the presence of Cassius, it was like her blood *knew* it was his, and she hated that.

She forced herself to turn away from his beautiful face, keeping her hands in the front pouch of Dallas's hoodie.

She had planned on going home immediately after she'd arrived back in Virginia, but it seemed fate had other plans for her. Once she'd parked the

Impala in the driveway, staring up at the dark, empty plantation house that now belonged to her, she could not bring herself to enter. She hated coming home from a case. Back to reality. So instead of walking up her steps, she'd walked down the driveway, with no destination in sight. Her feet led her to walking the streets of Chester in the rain, trying to avoid what was now her home. It didn't feel like home, though Ava was not sure what home really was anymore. Home was once Salem, Massachusetts, when life was perfect, happy.

Until vampires took everything from her.

Malcolm, her brother had divulged as much only after he'd realized she'd been bitten, and she couldn't help but fall into a spiral of painful thoughts every time she thought of them. Home was a dorm she'd left behind, and motels and hotels she'd crashed in on the road whilst helping her brother and his Goon Squad hunt vampires and other creatures of the night.

Now that her guardian, Becky Lee Michaels, had passed, leaving the magnificent property to Ava, she felt truly alone. Her brother had made being a hunter his top priority, forever searching for the vampires who had killed their parents and a way to clear Ava of the mark.

*Cassius's mark.*

Malcolm had made it more than clear that while her backup was helpful at times, he was adamant that she keep 'the fort down' in his absence, which was he nonchalant way of sitting her at the kids table. Even though they were no longer children. After all, she was twenty-three years old, she could more than take care of herself, and she'd proved that on numerous occasions.

Now going home to her inherited plantation home, complete with a pseudo-parent housekeeper, just made her feel small, insignificant. It was a stark reminder that Ava was alone. She hadn't had a real relationship since her college boyfriend, Ross, who'd unceremoniously ended up dead by vamps. She would have met the same fate, had it not been for Cassius... which she did not want to think about.

Ava had not known at the time when the angelic faced vampire asked her permission, what he truly meant. She only knew in that moment as she lay bleeding out on the floor that she would have agreed to anything if it meant she would live. She had not known the cost for such things. Aside from the demonologist, Sam Kingsley—who had turned out to be possessed by an incubus, and an alcohol infused makeout with Sawyer Thorne, the closest thing she had to a relationship was... whatever she had with Dallas, her brother's partner, and even that was sparse. After all, Dallas was just as much a nomad as her brother. When they'd discussed their arrangement only two years ago, she'd been more than fine with such things.

No attachment meant no pain.

She'd told herself it was better to be alone, a sentiment her brother echoed. Even Dallas himself had said the very same—*If you had no one, no one could hurt you.* But Ava was a Crowley, and she was restless, always searching for something. A way to break a bond. Strong arms to know when to hold her and when to let her go.

So why was standing in front of a vampire she longed to kill—who she could not bring herself to do so—the only place she could be still?

"Are you working a case?" Cassius said as he slowly ambled forward, nodding for her to follow him. To walk with him.

Ava knew trusting Cassius was dangerous. He was suave and attractive, and his proximity lit her blood on fire while giving her goosebumps at the same time.

But he was a monster.

A blood-eating, undead creature who would kill her himself if she was not careful.

She knew she should walk away. Go home as she had planned, but her bed was cold without Dallas to make her forget about the things that haunted her.

Jake Dallas had a way of exorcising her demons that she was certain no one else would ever match. His brand of love was not love at all, but a perpetual war. A macabre dance over hellfire, and she was never certain which of them would escape alive when she was with him, a sentiment she'd relished at the beginning of their *arrangement,* but now had started to feel trapped by.

So, Ava followed Cassius as he led her down the street, like a moth to a flame.

"I just finished a case. Guess it's time to go back to my boring ass life," she said in disdain. She stole a glance at the vampire next to her, noticing he was dressed in a long, leather trenchcoat and boots. She had to admit the outfit was a departure from his normal grey shirt, black leather pants, and low-top converse tennis shoes, and it wasn't a bad look on him. Amidst the grey fog and the rain, he looked every bit an evil vampire come to drag her to hell.

*Why is that sexy?*

*Because it's the fucking bond.*

*It makes him appeal to you because that's what he needs to fucking end you.*

*You to be smitten with him.*

Was she smitten with him?

She wasn't sure, and the way her

heart lifted at the possibility forced her to push down the thought.

That would be insane, after all.

"I would hardly call your life boring," he said with a smirk.

"You're right. Your life is probably a lot more boring than mine. Surprised you haven't thrown yourself off a fucking cliff yet out of insanity."

"Of course not. I'd hate to rob you of the chance to slay me," he said as a small laugh escaped his throat. The sound was... kind of sexy, if she was being honest. Her insides fluttered and she looked away. They had come to the library. It was only four years ago, they stood here and he had divulged he was a vampire.

She hadn't believed his words, but her blood knew the truth.

*I should have killed him then.*

She'd vowed to slay him if he didn't stay away from her, and she hadn't even come into her slayer training yet. She'd only known with every fiber of her being that he would be the death of her, vampire or not, and such a thing was just as frightening a concept as the reality that monsters existed.

"You make it sound like you're looking forward to your inevitable demise," she said as the rain suddenly stopped. The light from the lamppost out front, and the low ceiling lights of the library, cast amber ribbons of reflections in the puddles between them. Cassius shifted his weight, his golden hair falling in his eyes. The light fell on him, making the raindrops in his golden hair shimmer, his bright emerald eyes imploring her gaze.

"Do not tell me you are not? You only threaten my very existence every time you see me."

"That's because you don't how to fucking leave me alone. Because you are a stalker." She was very flustered at his words and her cheeks felt warm.

"Perhaps I like your company."

"Wow. Does that kind of thing really work for you, Cas?" she bit.

"I beg your pardon?" he asked.

"Nevermind. I should probably be going..." She sighed and turned toward the direction of home.

"Ava..." he called out to her, his voice full of something she'd certainly never heard before.

"Go home, Cas." She waved at him as she walked away, though she had to admit a part of her wished he'd reject her plea and run beside her, insisting on seeing her home safely. That he'd walk her up her steps, as he had many other times, leaving her at her door.

Or that he'd show up in her room, climbing in through her window just as she'd awaken from a bad dream.

But Cassius did not chase after her, and that made her feel a mixture of sadness and relief.

When Ava had reached her large plantation home, she breathed a sigh of relief as she opened the door. She locked it immediately, flicking on the light, and the silence was deafening, and her heart heavy.

*Fucking hell.*

She pulled her hood down, and headed straight for the fridge. She'd been gone a week, and had told Connie, her aunt's housekeeper—now her housekeeper—not to worry about cleaning, or stocking the fridge. When she opened it, she could see the Chinese woman had not regarded her request. The refrigerator was stocked with all her favorite things, including a bottle of Bordeaux.

Ava did not truly care for red wine, she much preferred a solid, hearty scotch or whiskey, but Cassius did. He'd mentioned it once, and she'd gone to purchase a bottle to see how awful it was, and she had to admit there was something about the bitterness that soothed her soul. And when she would undoubtedly awaken in a cold sweat from the memories that haunted her in her nightmares to a golden-haired, green eyed angel of death, she longed for its bitterness.

Ava poured a glass of wine, pausing for a moment as she closed her eyes, wrapping her fingers around the glass. Her cell phone vibrated against her ass, and she let out a breath she did not realize she had been holding.

She slid the phone out of her pocket, opening her eyes. The artificial light of her phone lit up the small space as she read the notification from the man she referred to as *Asshole* in her phone.

Jake Dallas.

*You up, kitten?*

She licked her lips as she took a sip of the bitter wine.

*You know I am. Otherwise you wouldn't be texting me.*

She took another sip of her drink as

she waited for his response.

*I miss you.*

Three small words.

How was it that three small words felt so heavy on her heart?

*Should I say it back?*

She did miss him, in a way. She missed the warmth of his body curled around her in the middle of the night, and she missed going head to head with him in a ring or a motel room. Hell, she even missed pushing his buttons and pissing him off.

She did not miss his voice, or his bipolar personality. One moment he was fine with their arrangement, and the next he was ignoring her, or running his hands through her hair, holding her in his lap and being... caring. It was exhausting keeping up with his fluctuating moods.

She'd been clear two years ago that she was not looking for a man to settle down with, or a boyfriend to bring to game night every week at the Third Eye. She had vowed not to get attached to anyone, and Dallas had been upfront with her, too. He wasn't looking for anything serious, either. He could not afford attachments with the lifestyle he'd become accustomed to. Hunting came first, and it always would. They'd agreed to keep it casual, after all, it was just sex.

*Really, really good sex at that.*

She let her thoughts drift. It didn't mean anything, and that was how she preferred it. It didn't change anything about their friendship, or their hunter partnership. Feelings were off the table.

But lately, these rare moments with Dallas were becoming more frequent, and Ava was not sure how to respond, or where things had changed.

*Did they change?*

She texted him back.

*Good to know.*

Ava took a long drink and refilled her glass before he had responded.

*Are you pissed at me?*

Ava rolled her eyes, letting out a frustrated laugh. For a thirty-five year old man, he was often quite dense.

*Not everything is about you, you know.*

It seemed an eternity until he'd responded.

*Are you trying to start an argument with me? I just wanted to let you know I was thinking about you.*

Just as soon as he'd sent the first text, another came.

*Don't you miss me?*

Ava pursed her lips, feeling a mixture of annoyance and anger. How dare he make her feel like the asshole. Clinger was not a good look on him.

*I can't miss you if you don't fucking go away,* Ava texted harshly.

She wasn't sure where the anger was coming from, but she didn't shy away from it. In fact, she embraced it. Anger was familiar, cathartic even.

*Is that what you want, Ava? For me to go away?*

Ava felt her stomach turn.

Is that what she wanted?

For him to leave her alone?

She wasn't sure. She only knew this conversation made her feel rather anxious. It felt too much like an argument with a boyfriend, and Dallas was certainly *not* her boyfriend.

For starters, no one knew about their relationship. Well, no one but her best friend, Ember, and she was not Dallas's biggest fan, either. They'd kept everything hush for the last two years, since they'd first crossed that line when she was only twenty, while on a case in the tiny mountain town of Mahoning, but if she was being truthful, whatever existed between her and Dallas had been going on much longer than that. It had all started when Cassius bit her four years ago, when Dallas became her mentor, her trainer, and the unattainable, emotionally unavailable, wishy-washy asshole she could never quite pin or quit instigating.

And the last two years had been a blur of sex and fighting, moments stolen in shitty motel rooms, bars, and even cars, and once on Dallas's motorcycle, when they weren't driving stakes into vamps like toothpicks in cheese.

Not once had Dallas shown up to her doorstep outside of a hunt, not even on Thanksgiving when Mal had come home, when he had done so before...

*Before we fucked.*

Ava drained the last of her drink before sending a final text.

*I want to go to bed. I think you should, too.*

She placed her glass in the sink before heading to her bedroom.

*Okay. Good night, Ava.*

Ava tossed her phone on the end table as she crawled into bed, curling atop her burgundy covers, feeling colder than ever, and she knew it wasn't because the window was open. The wind whistled outside, and she felt overwhelmed with sadness.

*Why am I like this?*

She closed her eyes tightly.

*Why do I push people away?*

The scar on her wrist heated, her skin prickling with goosebumps, and she couldn't help but feel a tightness in her chest. Though, when she looked up, Cassius was nowhere to be found, and the feeling had disappeared, and that hurt her heart most of all.

# CHAPTER FOUR

CASSIUS STROLLED THROUGH the parking lot of the Willow Creek Morgue, feeling rather famished. It was now Tuesday, and the last two nights had been practically torturous.

Jasmine and Taijiri had decided to stay a bit longer wherever they were, since Cassius did not press for details when Taijiri had texted him. His friend had only said he wished to spend some 'quality time' with his companion and Cassius could not fault him for such things, though a part of him was jealous that Taijiri had a companion to spend time with in the first place.

It had been ages since Cassius had been with another. His life of solitude had been more than deliberate. After Eden had exposed her true colors, after she'd admitted her hand in his father's death, among so many others of those he held dear, it was the final straw. They'd been strained for years, trying to keep up their rouse, their engagement. And he had *tried* so very hard to be the man Eden needed, but alas, she had no room in her heart for him. He could not compete with the ghost of the only man she truly loved, Marcellus. And despite his pure bloodline and his genetic ability to reproduce with mortals and vampires alike, they had not managed to do what their union was intended for.

Once he'd discovered the truth about her miscarriage, about how she'd *used* him as nothing more than a pawn to cover up the truth, he knew there was nothing left in his heart for the vicious Eden Boracelli. With her admission, she'd taken the last remains of any feelings he'd harbored for her.

Cassius had spent the last few decades in hiding, knowing that Eden would not take no for an answer. She'd tried to thrall him from leaving all those years ago, after all, realizing she was far too late. Even now, Cassius hated to think about everything—no, *everyone*— he had left behind.

At the time, Eden had moved up in

rank, and was one of the Boracelli Queen's closest allies. He'd agreed with Francesca's proposal, to be betrothed and united with Eden because of the sins of his father, and the need to protect his mother.

The Boracellis demanded an Aurelian stud.

After his father had left the high covens altogether, running away with his mother so they could live their life in exiled happiness, they were left to make arrangements with covens who did not possess such pure bloodlines. And with his father dead, without his protection, his mother was exposed and fair game. He'd agreed to the arrangement for her.

His mother had offered him and his seed up in exchange for protection from Lucious Aurelia's enemies. And though it had angered him, made him feel as if he was nothing more than a prize pony on the auction block, he could not throw his mother to the wolves. He would always protect her, the woman who gave up everything to have him. When he'd left without word to anyone but Leon, his closest friend, he'd left her, too.

*It was better she did not know what I planned...*

He still felt remorse. Cassius did not miss much of his life prior to his arrival in Chester, but he did miss his mother, and often he wondered if she was still alive, kept in the halls of the Boracelli castle still to this day, and if she was happy, if she was all right.

Cassius pushed through the door, smoothing his hair back as he came to the front desk. His stomach felt so hollow, and the pain was maddening. His throat was parched. Just the sight of the woman at the desk made his mouth water, knowing her blood would be fresh and warm, but Cassius had mastered a level of control over the years that would drive Eden to drink. The woman who claimed to be in control all the time was a slave to impulsivity, and she had the body count to show for it.

"Can I help you?" she asked with a bored sigh.

"I'm here to see Bryan. We are... meeting for lunch," Cassius said with a well practiced smile that hid just enough of his fangs that he could pass for a human.

This song and dance wasn't one he practiced often anymore, he'd grown rather accustomed to his routine corpse blood delivery, and therefore, crashing a morgue was a thing of the past for Cassius. He hadn't done so in two years, not since he'd been in Oklahoma to help Leon clear his name after he"d come under investigation for murders that he had no part in.

*Murders committed by an incubus, no less.*

Though the experience had been refreshing, the blood he'd consumed had not been. It had been laced with incubus toxin, and had thrown him into a lust-filled haze. It had been a miracle he'd had enough control not to throw Ava up against the vending machine in the Silver Starling hotel and ravish her until she begged to be bitten.

Cassius pushed the memory away.

*No, that is not who you are.*

"Oh, I guess he must not have called you, either," the woman, a short, petite teal haired woman spoke.

"I beg your pardon?" Cassius asked, his voice going flat. He did not like the sound of this.

"Bryan didn't show up today. No call or anything. I hope he's okay. Boss said if he doesn't hear from him by tomorrow, they might have to do a welfare check or something."

Cassius's blood chilled, his thoughts immediately turning dire. Bryan was, if anything, a stickler for routine. Since his first brush with death—where Cassius had saved him from a vampire in the woods—he'd become highly reclusive. His job in the coroner's office provided him the means to supply Cassius with a steady supply of corpse blood as a return favor, but it was usually quite an isolated job. The man had become something of an occultist, a mad scientist since his brush with death—and aside from his return favors, Bryan kept his distance from Cassius.

*Most humans with a sense of self preservation are smart to stay away from monsters.*

His melancholy would have to wait, though, because suspicion was driving the boat right now, and Cassius knew he needed more information. His guilt and despair would always be there, swimming just beneath the surface of his cold, pale skin.

"I am sure it must have slipped his mind, you know how hyper-focused he can be sometimes," Cassius said, using his smile, and only an ounce of his thrall to flood the woman, preventing her from asking too many questions.

Her eyes glazed a bit as she looked at him, her demeanor shifting to more flirtatious and wanting.

"But I'm not doing anything for lunch, if you need some company," she said with a giggle.

"I'm afraid that won't be necessary. But thank you for the offer," he said as she nodded, sighing. Cassius pulled back on his thrall as he waved her goodbye, and walked out into the fog-laden afternoon toward the woods.

As he came to the clearing, he heard a rustle in the bushes. Pausing for a moment, he was hit with a wave of hunger that made his stomach tighten. It seemed using his thrall on the woman, even if it was only for a short moment, had only exacerbated his thirst. A cold sweat formed on his brow as images flooded him. Of fangs in neck, of the memory of blood on his tongue. But not just any blood.

*Her blood.*

*Ava's.*

Cassius let out a groan of defeat, feeling his cock twitch from the memory. He hated that even now, the memory itself could awaken such desire in him. Ava was so much more than his perfect feast. She was feisty, sarcastic, and rough around the edges, but he'd had the privilege of catching the woman beneath the armor when she thought he wasn't looking, or when she'd let her guard down.

The woman who tried to fight him for his donut when she had a dozen of her own, or who offered him her umbrella, while her pulse raced, insinuating it was just 'polite'. The woman who listened to music too loud so no one would know she was singing along. The woman who suffered from nightmares and tried to stifle them with wine, whiskey, and men like Jake Dallas, who would never understand the gift she truly was.

Cassius adjusted himself, trying to shake off the thoughts. As he did so, a deer appeared in the clearing. Cassius watched its ears twitch as it looked at him, and he did not think.

For, he couldn't.

He could only act on impulse, starved as he was, and closed the distance. Cassius moved with lightning speed, chasing the doe into the woods, cornering her until he was certain he was out of sight. He could never be too careful. He'd gotten this far keeping his nose clean and under the radar, he did not wish to risk it now. Not when he was so very hungry. The hunter inside of him—no, the *monster* inside of him—reared to the surface as Cassius caught the doe in his hands. She looked up at him with pleading eyes, scared out of her wits, and he hated himself.

He hated that his need for blood prevailed over everything else, and that after only two days of no corpse blood, he was here in this forest, with a frightened animal between his hands.

"I'm so sorry about this," he whispered, feeling the shame and guilt mix with his hunger, his need. His predatory instinct. Cassius did not waste a moment as he brought his fangs down on the deer's neck, holding its body still as it tried to fight him, tried to kick out of his grasp.

But he was stronger than an average human, and as Leon had once disclosed, stronger than the average vampire.

Warm blood hit his tongue, and it was sour and bitter. Cassius felt his gag reflex kick in, and he was disgusted with himself and the taste.

It wasn't like *real* blood. It wasn't even like corpse blood, which he had grown accustomed to.

He drank with a shudder, letting the gamey, slick blood slide down his throat, and he felt better. Better enough that his stomach had settled, though he knew it wouldn't be for long.

It'd been nearly fifty years since he'd had fresh blood, save for that night four years ago whence he'd tasted Ava's once he bit her.

He'd subsisted on corpse blood solely, breaking into morgues and crematoriums like a criminal until he'd met Bryan. The urge to feast on animal blood had not been a prevalent one, as Cassius had discovered in his earlier years, it made him ill.

Cassius let go of the body of the deer, and it slumped to the ground, lifeless. He backed away as reality hit him, and found himself up against a tree. He closed his eyes and let the shame, the guilt, rise to the surface.

His thoughts wandered to Ava and her sweet blood, her bite, and her thriving pulse that was alive in his veins. Even if she did not care for him, even if she found him appalling and a thorn in her side, Cassius could not deny that being in her presence soothed the demons inside of him that would not let him be.

He opened his eyes, wiping the back of his hand over his mouth, as the first wave of nausea hit him.

*So much for a satisfying meal.*

Only a monster was capable of such things, and how could anyone love a monster?

# CHAPTER FIVE

THE DOOR BELL jingled, alerting Ava that a customer had finally decided to show up. She groaned as she shut her book, *East Anglian Witches & Wizards*, readying to have to put on her customer face and be chipper, friendly.

When she saw the customer in question sauntering in with a fresh coffee and a bag of something that smelled like a cherry danish from The

Mean Bean, though, she wasn't sure if she was relieved or annoyed. Perhaps a bit of both.

"Well, look what the cat dragged in this afternoon," she drawled as she leaned against the back counter, following Cas's graceful stride to her counter. He gingerly set the bag of pastry deliciousness down, pushing it to her like some offering to a caged, vicious animal.

"I need your help," he said as he set the coffee down next to it. On the other side of the counter, he stood perfectly still, looking at his offerings, then at her.

Waiting.

Ava narrowed her eyes and her stomach growled. She was not much of a morning person, and therefore, nine times out of ten, she rarely ate breakfast at home. Ava's idea of breakfast was coffee on the run. She could never wake herself early enough to leave the house in time to make it to the Mean Bean to eat something substantial, and she hated cooking first thing in the morning when she was barely awake. If she'd had any time, it was for a bowl of cereal, and this morning she'd had difficulty waking.

For the third night in a row, the nightmares had persisted. Ava had tossed and turned, never quite finding a modicum of comfort as her mind raced against her, not wanting to fall back into the darkness and the awful memories that awaited her.

*Ross's scream of terror.*

*Her parents bloodied bodies on the floor.*

*Sam Kingsley being exorcised.*

*A large, heavy werewolf with its jaws at her throat.*

*Being wrapped up in a vampire's thrall.*

She leaned forward, only enough to pull the brown paper bag off the counter, rifling it open only to catch a divine whiff of cherries, cream, and flaky sugar pastry.

*Cherry danish, my favorite.*

She regarded Cas as she broke off a small piece of the confectionary delight and chewed on it, wondering if this was some sort of trick. Cassius was many things, but he was not one to ask favors, especially from her.

Was it some sort of trap?

Was this how he got her?

Lured in with breakfast and glowing green emerald eyes?

Was she that easy?

"What the hell do you need my help with?" she said through a mouthful of danish. The tart cherry filling on her tongue was still warm, and it was rather delicious.

"It's Bryan."

Ava stilled for a moment. There weren't many things she and Cassius had in common; in fact she doubted they had much in common other than their mutual contact, Bryan.

She'd been working a case, one of her own, when she'd come across Bryan's services. The beautiful bloodsucker had urged her to visit the man, who was something of a laboratorial genius when it came to antidotes, potions, and preventative measures. If one needed dead man's blood, or a crystal to force a demon into, or protection oils, Bryan was capable of whipping up the best.

He was also a bit eccentric, but Ava knew beggars could not be choosers. It was not as if Chester had a white pages for hunter-adjacent occultists who you could rely on in a pinch.

"What about him?" Ava pressed.

Cassius leaned his arms on the counter.

"I think he may be in trouble. He is missing," Cassius stated sternly.

Ava shrugged. "Maybe he finally went off the deep end."

"He did not show up for work today. My gut tells me something is amiss."

Ava set the bag of half-eaten pastry down. Something about Cassius's tone felt off. He sounded legitimately worried.

But why would he be worried about

Bryan?

It wasn't like they were friends or anything. Ava pushed the thought down, feeling the strange impulse to soothe the vampire's worry.

"Maybe he's just not feeling well."

"I went by his residence as well. He is not there."

"You went inside?" Ava asked, surprised. "I mean, maybe he's just you know... indisposed with the flu or something. Wrapped up in a blanket burrito."

"No. I did not, but I knocked. No answer. From what I was able to discern, he was not there. I could see through the door window. The house looked... unkempt."

"You didn't just like... break in..." Ava suggested as she reached for the coffee.

"I am a lot of things, my sweet Avarice, but a locksmith I am not."

Ava rolled her eyes. "I mean, it's not that hard. Just a wiggle here and a pinch there..."

Cassius's eyes lit up as she licked her fingers clean of the sticky danish icing. She did not miss the way his gaze fell to her lips, how he fixated on her slender fingers as she licked them. He let out a breath as he licked his own lips before meeting her gaze. Something about the way he looked at her made her blood boil beneath the surface.

"Perhaps you could..."

"Are you asking me to break into a man's home?" Ava said with a smirk. Cassius pursed his lips.

"I suppose I am," he said plainly.

Ava sighed as she looked at the clock.

"Guess I'm going to lunch early," she said, taking a sip of her coffee. The perfect mix of cream and espresso made her insides flush, and her heart flutter with excitement as she grabbed the rest of the bag of danish, tucking it beneath her arm as she grabbed her cross-body purse, reaching for the store keys.

Cassius stood back while she readied herself, and she could keenly feel his gaze on her. She turned away just as she felt a blush creeping into her cheeks.

*What the hell is wrong with me?*

She stormed past Cassius, and he followed without question. He squeezed through the door after her, the narrow passageway causing him to brush against her, and the touch, as innocent as it was, made Ava stop dead in her tracks, key in the lock.

It wasn't the first time she'd ever *felt* him, though it had been quite a long time since she had. She could still remember the night he saved her life, how he'd taken her wrist in his hand, how his fingers brushed over her skin. Though the memory brought forth a myriad of other touches, other sensations she wanted to forget.

*His fangs piercing her skin, his tongue on her flesh.*

*The pure bliss of being in his thrall.*

Ava swallowed harshly, forcing the haunting memories away. She hated how they had a mind of their own, and filled her psyche so often. Especially, when she was alone, with no one to make her forget, and no one to satisfy her burning desires, the ones she tried to lock deep within.

Cas's body against hers sparked a fire in her blood, in her nerves. The feeling of his chest against her back, his stomach against her waist, caused her stomach to flip and a warmth to blossom between her thighs.

Ava angled herself away from his sight, feeling her cheeks flush once more.

*Jesus Christ!*

*This should not be happening!*

She chastised herself, locking the door and scurrying away to the curb where her car was parked.

Cassius stood on the side of the street, looking like some Calvin Klein model in his signature grey shirt and leather pants, all glowing green emerald eyes and golden hair blowing in the chilly Chester wind.

Ava folded herself into the driver seat, unlocking the passenger door from the inside. She swallowed as she stared at him from inside the car, feeling as if this crossed some sort of invisible line.

But the prospect of a case was much more enticing.

"Well, don't just stand there, get in," she grumbled as Cassius stared back at her.

He shook his head, obviously shoving away his own random thoughts or daydreams. If he thought this was how he would take her, feast on her blood and kill her, he had another thing coming. Ava's Impala was more secure than Fort Knox. Not only was she equipped with at least two stakes on her person, she kept a multitude of elixirs and weapons stashed all throughout the car. Her brother and Dallas had taught her well.

Cassius opened the door, angling himself in slowly, and Ava's blood heated as she watched him do so. The motion drew attention to his long, slender, leather covered legs.

She turned around, not wanting to stare at the beautiful monster any longer.

Ava started the car, and sped off quickly, in search of danger once more.

# CHAPTER SIX

CASSIUS WAS NO stranger to getting in cars with beautiful women, and it certainly wasn't the first time he'd been in Ava's Impala. It was, however, the first time he'd been invited inside without a second thought, and that notion made him feel some sort of mix of confusion and hope.

*Do not be silly, it has everything to do with Bryan and nothing to do with you.*

For a moment, Cassius could have sworn as he got in the car that Ava was blushing, though she'd turned away too quickly for him to be sure. But it did not matter. The racing pulse beneath his skin was more than evidentiary, and he could not help the twitch of a smile on his face.

Ava could deny many things, but she could not deny her blood, her racing pulse.

Ava turned up the radio, focusing her sight on the road intently. The crooning sounds of a man singing about looking for something he could not seem to find—or rather someone who evaded him every time he tried to find her—filled the space as Ava grumbled, changing the station.

"I liked that song," Cassius said, if

only to try and lighten the mood in the car. He could not shake the feeling that something was amiss with his lost friend. He had a bad feeling in his gut, but he was not one to jump to conclusions. Perhaps they would arrive at Bryan's humble abode just as he was pulling in. Perhaps his friend had a reasonable explanation for not showing up today. Perhaps Cassius had overreacted, let his imagination get the best of him.

"You don't even know who Nick Jonas is," Ava bit.

"Does that matter? I thought the sound was... soothing."

Ava rolled her eyes as she turned down the street.

"I mean, yeah, sure, if breathy heartthrobs with purity rings in need of a fucking haircut is your thing..." She turned down another street, entering the patch of forest that would soon take them to Bryan's house, every second like an eternity between them.

"Unless you're really a teenage girl in disguise," she said with a laugh.

Cassius could not help but rise to her bait.

"I can assure you I am neither a teenager or a girl."

"Could have fooled me with your ballerina leather tights and your floppy california bob." She giggled.

The sound was beautiful and rare. It was almost as if in that moment, she was... comfortable.

But before Cassius could grasp it, the moment slipped through his fingers like grains of sand in the hourglass when

Ava pulled up to Bryan's... home.

The shipping container-style residence was sleek and sophisticated and rather isolated. Against the foggy onset of mid-afternoon, it looked almost heinous. Threatening even.

*How could anyone truly live here?*

Ava exited the car without warning.

Casius shook his head, dispelling the stolen moment for good as he walked slowly behind Ava who was now digging around in her trunk, opening boxes, and bags, and...

"Aha! There you are! Damn little fucker thought it could escape, but no way! Not today Satan..." Ava tucked a leather pouch underneath her arm, the sound of leather upon leather filling the silence.

Cassius moved to shut the trunk, and

Ava nearly jumped five feet off the ground.

"What the fuck are you doing?" she said, her guard up once more.

Cassius fought a frown, remembering only mere moments ago when she hadn't been so brash.

"I just thought..."

She focused her eyes as she slammed the trunk, causing Cassius to jump back, if only to avoid getting shut in the trunk with the rest of her slaying paraphernalia.

"You thought wrong," she bit, leaving him in her dust as she headed for Bryan's front door. She looked around the front of the yard—if the dried grass and unkempt pile of weeds could be called a yard to begin with—before sliding the leather pouch out from under her arm.

"The coast is clear, Ava. I do not think we will be disturbed."

Ava scoffed at him as she pulled out what looked like a long, slender metal toothpick with a curve at the end. The metal tool reminded Cassius of an instrument he'd seen long ago, and one that had nor provided relief to anyone it touched. He shuddered at the memory.

"Yeah, well, don't take it personal, Cas. I only trust my own fucking judgment, okay?" she said through her breath as she kneeled in front of Bryan's door, angling the pick inside. She let it rest in the lock as she turned her attention to the remaining tools in the pad.

Cassius watched as she concentrated, laying them out on the

pavement, selecting them like a surgeon selects his scalpel.

"Of course. I understand." He nodded as she selected her tool and started working. The motion of her tweaking the tools together looked almost like crocheting, and Cassius had to fight a laugh as an image of Ava knitting black lace doilies with curse words came to mind.

"All right, and... I think I'm in," she said as a small click sounded.

Cassius watched her stand, noting the motion drew attention to her rather long, sinful legs. Even in jeans they looked to stretch for miles, and he did not miss the opportunity to trace over her lithe form.

She gently pushed open the door, and for a moment time stood still. There they were on the edge of Bryan's doorstep. At this proximity, he could smell the lingering scent of jasmine and bergamot, feel the heat radiating from her body like a bonfire.

The desire to reach out and touch her, to set his hand at the small of her back and run his nose up her neck and through her hair, to breath in her floral, seductive scent was too much to bear, and so Cassius reached his finger tips out, but they would not make contact with their target.

They would only grasp at the nothing, at the faint breeze left behind as Ava wasted no time, heading into the shadows of Bryan's home, into the unknown once more.

# CHAPTER SEVEN

AVA HAD BEEN to Bryan's modular home a handful of times over the last two years.

After TerrorCon, she'd come across the squirrely man while working a local case in which she'd thought vamps were responsible, but it only turned out to be a group of bored teenagers messing with spirits. Though it was out of her wheelhouse of fanged creatures, Ava had always been interested in all the facets of the occult and did not waste the chance to learn upfront about spirit possession, and how to prevent such things.

Cassius had been there that night, with a steaming cup of coffee by her car after she'd learned vamps were not to blame. It was almost as if he knew somehow exactly where she'd be, which both irritated her and, if she was being honest, made her feel a sense of relief. It made her feel less alone, even if she would not say it out loud.

He offered her a cup of coffee and a contact when she'd admitted her search turned up no vampires to slay, but rather stupid teenagers who'd bitten off more than they could handle.

Cassius led her to Bryan that evening, an eccentric man living in a shipping container passing as a modular house, who looked exactly like the kind of man who would live on the outskirts of society with the brain to match such isolated things. Ava was not certain why a vampire would have such a contact as Bryan, though, someone who was well versed in occult elixirs and preventatives. It wasn't like Cassius needed elixirs or preventatives for anything.

He was a vampire, what use would he have for a possession potion?

Vampires couldn't be possessed.

Only the living could be possessed.

In the times Ava had visited Bryan, he hadn't been the cleanest human, but there was an order to his chaos and she appreciated his eccentricities. But now, as she stood in his living room, the overhead lights turning on of their own accord, buzzing with ominous flickering to accompany the ambiance and the severity of the situation, Ava felt her heart sink.

The place was a wreck, more so than normal.

"Holy fuck," Ava grumbled as she made her way across the floor, through a small smattering of strewn papers. Cassius's footsteps sounded behind her, soft and slow. As if he was trying to keep his distance.

*Good.*

*He should stay the hell away.*

She thought the thoughts instinctively, but her heart lurched at the bitterness of them.

Did she want him to stay away?

She was not entirely certain the

answer was yes, given the fact she'd damn near lept at the chance to investigate Bryan's disappearance with the gorgeous monster. But Ava could not lose herself in the labyrinth of thoughts Cassius usually brought upon her with his presence, and she pushed them aside. She would deal with them later.

"It does look a little chaotic in here," he agreed as he turned away from Ava, heading toward the kitchen area, which doubled not just as a kitchen, but Bryan's alchemical lab.

"It looks like a bomb went off," she said as she stopped in front of his desk, staring at his computer. She gingerly pushed around papers on the surface, not quite sure what she was looking for, but knowing that whatever it was she would know it when she saw it.

"Be careful what you touch, you don't want your fingerprints on anything," Cassius called as he opened and shut cabinets.

"What's the matter, Cas? Worried they'll whisk me away into a cage where you can't get me?" She smirked, turning around to look at the vampire, whose face had gone cold. His green eyes were blank, as if he was remembering some unpleasant memory, and he looked away.

"There is nowhere you could go that I would not find you," he murmured and Ava's skin prickled with goosebumps, her blood boiling just beneath the surface at the darkness of his tone.

"God, you are a grade A creeper, you know that?" She shook her head, pulling her hand into her leather jacket sleeve before touching the ON button to Bryan's computer.

"What are you doing?" Cassius asked, slightly panicked.

"Um, if CSI has taught me anything with its reruns, it's that there's always a cyber trail."

"I told you not to touch anything," he huffed.

"I didn't touch it! I used my jacket! But if you're so fucking worried, then maybe you should get over here and start fingerprinting up everything. I doubt you're in the system, being the ancient pain in the ass you are. Unless, of course, you've been moonlighting as a serial killer or something," she said as she narrowed her eyes at him.

Cassius scoffed, closing a cabinet rather harshly and Ava cracked a small smile.

*So I can piss him off.*

*Noted.*

Cassius sauntered over to her, the flickering lights casting shadows on his features and making him look far more threatening than normal. With his hands in his leather pants pocket, golden hair falling in front of those glowing green eyes, he looked like the villain from one of those 1920s film noir flicks her Aunt Becky used to be so gung-ho over.

Ava took in the sight of him like this, and she did not miss the way it made her blood boil, made her stomach flip. Memories of the first time he'd emerged from the shadows played on repeat in her brain, and she had to swallow the compulsion to *sigh*. To fall into the aura, the thrall of the vampire who'd saved her life, and could not for the undead life of himself, seem to stay away from her.

She turned around, facing the computer which had started up, knocking some papers off the desk.

Cassius caught them with ease, with perfect timing.

*He's so fucking extra.*

One glance at the paper, and Ava did a double take.

"What the hell is this?" she said as she grabbed the paper off of him.

"Ava..."

The crinkled paper touted an upcoming event in Albright, Ohio, a town she'd certainly never heard of. The flyer boasted a rather haunting looking house in black and white, with text that read *Marquis Masquerade & Fun House: Where your darkest desires and your worst nightmares come to play.*

"What is it?" Cass asked as he leaned his head over her shoulder. The proximity made her skin flush, her blood race. This close, she could smell his natural, spicy scent. It wasn't something she often thought about, except in the dead of a lonely night where the thoughts had become too much to bear. When there was only one way to quiet them, where she could let the memory of his warm, wet tongue on her skin mix with the memory of his scent, his touch, and the sharpness of his fangs piercing her skin until she'd brought herself to release, before the guilt and shame took over.

"A hunch," she said as she looked at the computer. "Check his history."

"I beg your pardon?" he asked, his

voice much breathier than usual in her ear.

Ava had to step away, for the sound caused a wetness to bloom between her thighs that was quite unwanted at this moment.

"I mean, you do know how to use a computer, right?" she taunted him, finding solace in the sarcasm.

This was easy, this was normal.

Cas breathing sexily in her ear was *not* normal, and her liking it was also not normal. So, she refused to acknowledge such things, shoving them down into the dungeon inside where she cast all thoughts of Cas to, the dark prison where she'd lock up such things and never let them out again.

"Of course I know how to use a computer. I frequented the university, too. I sat in on many lectures and classes."

"Aww, how cute. The old man learns basic computers 101. Did they teach you how to browse a user's history or did they just stop at email because the rest was too difficult?" she said with a laugh.

Cassius pursed his lips as he nudged her aside, moving his fingertips on the touchpad.

Ava watched as he brought up the browser successfully and accessed the history. She had to admit she was kind of... impressed.

*Maybe he can be useful after all.*

"You were saying, my sweet Avarice?" He smirked.

Ava leaned closer to the screen, scanning Bryan's somewhat questionable search history. It seemed

Bryan favored the darkweb and two singles sites. AltGothGirls.Com and GothBabes4ME. She pointed to the screen on one of the GothBabes4ME links.

"Bring that up, please," she ordered, and Cassius did as she asked without hesitation. Ava shook her head as a small smile crossed her face.

"Bryan, you little fucking pervert," she said with a laugh. The website displayed a rather drunken looking picture of Bryan and his GothBabes4ME profile. Under the listings of his preferences, Ava couldn't help but giggle, or the comments left on his page.

"Scroll down," she said through a giggle.

"What is so funny?" Cassius asked, but he did so all the same.

"Just... I mean... I guess I didn't think Bryan was like... looking for someone... I guess."

"Is not everyone looking for someone?" Cassius's voice was smooth, even. Like warm chocolate cake straight from the oven.

Ava felt her heart catch in her throat as she stole a glance at him.

*What the fuck is wrong with me?*

"Some people like to be alone. I thought Bryan was one of them."

Cassius's voice softened. "No one *wants* to be alone."

Ava's stomach twisted at his admission. She almost felt a sting of sympathy for the monster.

*Monster.*

Ava had to remember that was what he was. A monster who feasted on the living, a wolf in sheep's clothing. And he would do the same to her if she was not careful.

"Stop!" she exclaimed as she saw a comment from a "Enchantress" on his page. The woman was breathtaking. Long, black hair and blue eyes and a silver nose ring stared at them. The woman had commented with an invitation to the Marquis Masquerade & Fun House, some sort of Labyrinth event. She had stated Bryan could message her with details on meeting up beforehand to discuss... *opportunities.*

"Check his DMs," Ava ordered.

Cassius swallowed harshly, looking lost in thought, but he did so.

*What is his deal?*

*He's acting weird today.*

The notion that Ava had come to

expect a certain way of behavior from the bloodsucker was startling and she did not want to think about the implications of such things. Instead, she watched as Cassius brought up Bryan's messages, and sure enough, she had her culprit.

*Enchantress* had messaged him with a location, a date, and a time.

"Motherfucking bingo," Ava said proudly.

"Care to clue me in on your epiphany, Mrs. Sherlock?" Cassius teased her.

"I mean, it's kind of obvious, isn't it? Baby Tim Burton over here fucked up and didn't follow the rules of internet meet ups. He probably went to go meet Enchantress, didn't tell anyone... I mean, like, who is he going to tell? You? Pfttt." She waved her hand in the air.

Cassius raised an eyebrow at her as

she continued her crime-drama worthy monologue.

"Then, he probably got up there and got fucking catfished and is sitting in Enchantress's—whoever they really are—in their basement somewhere tied up and gagged."

"You have deduced all of this from a flyer and some DMs?" Cassius asked, stroking his chin. The slow, rhythmic motion of his fingers made Ava's blood rush.

"I mean, it's a theory."

"It is a good theory. What do you suggest we do next?"

"What is it with you and this *we* crap? I told you, Cassius. There is no we."

"So, I suppose I should just embark to Ohio myself, and leave you to your devices and your riveting life as it were. I understand," he said as he gingerly pulled the flyer from her hands.

Ava stared at it, feeling as if she was once again crossing an invisible line, pushing past the pit of snakes in Indiana Jones' Temple of Doom. There would surely be another booby trap waiting for her on the other side of the pit, but what was one more in the grand scheme of treasure?

A man's life may very well be at stake, and what if Cassius took more lives on said trip?

No, she needed to go to see this through, to rescue Bryan and to make sure Cassius didn't sink his fangs anywhere they did not belong.

"Fuck you. I'll have you know I'm off until Monday from my *riveting job,*" she bit.

Cassius smiled, showing just a hint of his fang, and Ava's insides turned to molten lava. She clenched her jaw, knowing the only way out was through.

"Then I take it *we* are going to Ohio to find our... Baby Tim Burton, as you called him?"

"I am going to Ohio. You can tag along, since, you know, you and Bryan are such fucking besties. I wouldn't want you to get your panties in a bunch and blow up my fucking phone while I try to save the day."

"You may need back up when you go in and save the day," Cassius smoothly said as Ava folded the flyer up and stuck it in her pocket.

"The day I ask you for back up will be a cold day in Hell, Cas," she grumbled as she headed for the door, wondering if she'd just signed her death certificate.

"When do we depart?" he called out, his voice oddly chipper.

Ava stopped in the doorway, turning around to look at him once more.

"I get off from work at eight, so eight thirty?" She said the words, but they felt heavy.

Ominous even.

"I shall meet you at your home at eight thirty, then," he said triumphantly.

She turned around, not bothering to look at him any longer. She needed to get the hell out of Bryan's apartment. Away from the prospect of a case, away from the sinfully delicious vampire who made her blood rush and her heart skip a beat.

# CHAPTER EIGHT

CASSIUS SMOOTHED HIS hair back as he neared the gate of Ava's residence.

Though he hadn't migrated to Chester until 1985, he'd certainly seen his fair share of plantation homes in the south when he and Eden had traveled along the eastern coast in the twenties, and he'd been in plenty of castles, mansions, and estates in his rather long life. But he'd never felt as nervous, as on the spot as he did at that moment as he walked through the gates to Ava's newly inherited digs.

It wasn't as if it was his first time seeing the place. He frequented it often, in fact; though most of the time he was sequestered to either the front porch or Ava's bedroom in the middle of the night when he did visit. On nights he couldn't sleep, he'd stroll by the estate until he was certain she was all right and then, he would retire to his favorite piano lounge until the place closed, drowning his sorrow, his memories, and his pesky desire to *hope* perhaps Ava would come around to their predicament.

*Predicament.*

That is what he was to her, something that happened to her that she did not agree to. Although, to be fair, she had agreed, but as Ava had reminded him on countless occasions, she hadn't truly known what she was agreeing to. The fine print had been evaded, because there was no time to waste. She was dying, and he had a way to save her, so he did.

And Cassius speculated bond or no bond, he would do the same if anything, or anyone threatened to put Ava Crowley into an early grave.

He took a breath as he made his way up her steps, standing in front of the door feeling as if he was crossing over into another dimension. One where upon the door opening, a beautiful, snarky slayer would look at him with bright eyes and a wicked grin, spout some sarcastic nonsense and invite him in—into her home, her heart, and her bed for all eternity.

He pushed the thoughts away, knowing they were dangerous, blaming such things on his recent corpse feeding. Blood always incited lust, it was just vampire biology. Nothing more.

Cassius had rationed breaking into the morgue was risky, even if there was no one currently working there at the time. Though it wasn't something he could keep doing, for regularly scheduled break ins would draw attention, and Cassius could not afford such things. He'd laid low, kept his nose clean, if only in an attempt to live outside the grasp of Eden, the high covens, and everything he'd left behind.

He hated skulking around like some criminal or some junkie in need of a fix, but the truth was rather simple. If

Cassius did not fill his stomach and feed the monster inside of him before embarking on a trip—no matter how short—he would be a danger to Ava. And as far as Cassius was concerned, that just could not happen. He would never put her in harm's way. Not now, not ever. They were bound by blood, for better or for worse.

The corpse blood was cold, as he'd had to pull it directly from the fridge, and it was not the best as far as taste. Later, he'd have to explain to Bryan about the missing logs, but it would be a small price to pay once they'd rescued the squirrely man and everyone made it through unscathed. At least, that was what he held onto, it was the outcome he hoped for. He wasn't sure he could face a much harsher reality.

Bryan had been gone for at least a day, if not longer, which was suspicious enough, but if Ava was right, and he was truly locked in someone's basement, then time was of the essence.

Cassius breathed a slow, deep breath as he balled his fist, and knocked on the door. His heart slowly thudded in his chest as it seemed like forever until the door was opened. But it was not Ava who greeted him, no. It was a tiny Chinese woman.

"Can I help you?" she asked sweetly, eyeing him up and down.

Cassius cleared his throat.

"Is Mrs. Crowley home?" he asked, feeling unsure of himself for a moment. Ava hadn't mentioned living with anyone, and he'd never seen any evidence otherwise, but then again, he hadn't spent much time anywhere but her bedroom in the middle of the night.

"And who may I ask is calling on *Mrs. Crowley,*" the woman said with a smirk. The potent smell of cinnamon and sugar wafted toward him, and his stomach twisted with recognition.

*Cookies.*

Cassius straightened his stance, looking the woman in the eyes poignantly. "My name is Cassius." He did not bother to give a last name, feeling on the spot. Such things held no value to him anymore. He'd been taught to keep his Aurelian heritage a secret, until he'd met Eden. He'd adopted her late husband's surname, Wright for a time, and she did not seem to mind his taking it then. Though the rouse of Cassius Wright had dissolved rather quickly whence he was spotted at a coronation for the Meidici's, another lineage of damn near vampire royalty. It wasn't long after that, the Boracellis had discovered his true bloodline, and Cassius Wright was put to rest until he'd joined forces with Eden again, when they'd been betrothed.

After fleeing Eden and the Boracellis, last names served no purpose. It would only make him easier to find, documented or not, and Cassius wished to be lost.

"Cassius, hmmm." The woman's eyes smiled, giving Cassius the impression she would not let him go if he stepped inside. "Well, Cassius, I am Constance Chen." She waved him in the door, and Cassius felt as if he was surely walking toward his inevitable death.

But if death included cookies and Ava Crowley, he would die a thousand times.

"Ava should be home soon..." She tutted as Cassius crossed the threshold into the Michaels estate.

Becky Lee Michaels, Ava's aunt, had been somewhat well known to the town. She had her hands in nearly every committee, every event. A single woman with no children, and no family left, Ava's aunt had amassed a wealth of her own in addition to the inheritance bestowed upon her.

Cassius knew Ava did not talk about her parents much, or her coming to Chester. In fact, their conversations mostly consisted of her reminding him she would kill him, or in some instances, details about the cases she'd taken on, or supernatural knowledge.

But Cassius wondered as he stood in the grand foyer of the estate, what had truly transpired to bring Ava and her brother to this haunting town, and why Ava had never mentioned a Constance Chen before.

"Feel free to have a seat," Constance gestured to the white sofa, and Cassius nodded, escaping his thoughts.

"Thank you, Mrs. Chen," he said graciously as he took his seat, setting his hands in his lap.

*Why am I so nervous?*

"Would you like a cookie?" she asked, her demeanor shifting from suspicious and deadly to sweet and caring in the blink of an eye.

"I would love that, actually." He politely nodded, smiling; careful to hide his fangs behind his lips. It was a feat he'd long mastered, and truly the only time he let them show was around Ava, and he only did so because he enjoyed knowing the effect it had on her, even if she did not admit it. Her pulse would *race* beneath his skin.

Constance Chen scuttled off to the kitchen and Cassius watched her do so. He took in the sight of the estate, all pale colors, white, and grey, and it reminded him of the Medici's estate in France.

*That was a lifetime ago, Cassius.*

*You need to forget such things...*

Constance set a small appetizer plate down before him on the glass coffee table, just as the front door opened.

"What the fuck?" Ava bit as she set her eyes on Cassius. He felt strangely warm under her viscous gaze.

"Ah, Ava, you are home..." Constance

tuttled.

"I said eight thirty," she growled, glancing from him to Constance.

"A gentleman is always early." Cassius smied.

Ava rolled her eyes.

"I swear one of these days I'm going to need a fucking restraining order," she said as she stormed up to them.

"You didn't have to invite him in, Connie." She huffed.

"Ava..." Constance sighed. Ava looked at the plate of cookies in front of him,

"God, and you're feeding him, too?" Her cheeks flushed, and he could tell she was most perturbed.

Cassius offered her the plate.

"Perhaps some sugar will soothe your frayed nerves," he said with a smirk.

Ava grabbed the cookies, clutching

the plate to her chest as she regarded him with a solid, heavy gaze.

"Don't fucking move. I will be out in five minutes. And don't harass my housekeeper."

*Housekeeper?*

"As you wish."

Ava rolled her eyes again, mumbling to herself as she stormed off, plate and all, toward her bedroom, leaving Cassius alone once more.

# CHAPTER NINE

AVA SHOVED A cookie in her mouth as she packed a bag. It was still warm, and the gooey chocolate relaxed her, if only a fraction.

She did not plan on being out of town long, but she knew the drive to Ohio would take at least five or six hours if they were making good time. Running on little sleep as it was, she was certain she'd have to find lodging accommodations somewhere at some point, even if it was only a few hours to sleep.

Bryan would have probably needed somewhere to rest as well, and the reality of just how little Ava knew the man made her feel slightly overwhelmed, but it was easier to focus on than anything else.

The thought of lodging with a vampire made her feel quite on edge, despite the fact Cassius regularly visited her bedroom.

In the middle of the night.

When she'd had nightmares.

She did not feel right throwing him out in the cold, or asking him to stay in the car, but at least if he was *near* her, she could account for him.

*And this is why you sleep with a*

*stake under your pillow.*

Ava threw a pair of jeans and some clean shirts in her bag. She knew it was rude of her to react the way she had earlier, not just to Cassius, but also to Connie. Connie did not know the danger she had put herself in, and therefore, she could not entirely blame the woman.

No, that blame had fallen on Ava.

Neither Mal or Ava had wanted to bring Connie into the fold, both vowing to keep the truth of what it was they got up to, hidden. But she certainly would not have lost her cool if Cassius had just listened to her instead of showing up ten minutes before she'd told him to be there.

Though to be fair, she would have been home sooner, had she closed the shop on time, which she would have had the pesky yoga-enthusiasts not shown up five minutes before close just to peruse the store and not actually buy anything.

Ava headed toward her armoire, opening it and taking stock of her weapons. She wasn't entirely sure what she would need, and it wasn't like the car wasn't stocked itself. A part of her knew she was just procrastinating and prolonging the inevitable. Bryan's disappearance likely had nothing to do with vampires or monsters, but she rationed one couldn't be too careful, or too prepared. She settled on grabbing an extra stake, some holy water reserve, and one of the decorated blades she'd bought earlier in the year from a guy on Craigslist who claimed it could kill anything undead. Perhaps she'd find out if it were true on this rescue mission.

She zipped up the bag hastily, throwing it over her shoulder. She grabbed another cookie, shoving it in her mouth, making quick work of eating.

They really did need to get moving.

When she'd come back out, she saw Cassius standing in front of the fireplace. His back was to her, and for a moment, Ava could imagine him somewhere regal, somewhere else than their present time. A mansion, a castle, or perhaps even a historical bed and breakfast, like some ghostly attractive inn keeper. Tall and slender, his silhouette stood out, his dark grey shirt, his pale skin and of course, those annoyingly sexy leather pants. Even his golden blond hair shimmered with sophistication.

Ava cleared her throat, gripping the strap to her duffel tighter as her blood rushed beneath the surface. They needed to leave.

Now.

Cassius turned as she cleared her throat. His green eyes glittered with excitement.

"Okay, so this train leaves right now," she barked as she headed toward the kitchen, to Connie, tapping her on the shoulder. Connie turned with a wicked smile.

"Cassius seems very nice, Ava."

Ava pursed her lips. "Yeah, well don't get any ideas. That's not going to happen, like ever. He's just a—"

What could she say?

*A vampire?*

*A pain in my ass?*

"A friend," she said the words, and they felt strange on her tongue. They felt... right.

Though she didn't really believe she and Cassius were friends. Friends meant you *liked* the person, and Ava did not *like* Cassius.

She was grateful he'd saved her life, but they had already settled the score, hadn't they?

"Well, it is nice to see you making friends, then," Connie said as she returned to her dishes.

"Connie, I... I'm going out of town for the weekend. I'll be back on Monday, okay? Don't worry about coming in or—"

Connie waved a sudsy hand at her. "Have a good time with your *friend*."

Ava nodded, if only because she wanted to end the conversation. She was starting to feel on the spot.

"Okay. Bye." She stood tall, turning around once more and exiting the kitchen toward the gorgeous vampire waiting at the door. As she approached, he smiled, showing just a hint of fang, and her stomach flipped.

He opened the door for her.

"After you, friend."

Ava rolled her eyes as she brushed past him.

"We are not friends, Cas. We are... co-workers, at best."

"Still, you did not call me your co-worker. You called me your *friend.*"

Ava huffed as she unlocked the door of the impala.

"Eavesdropping was once a punishable crime, you know," she bit.

He only had the audacity to look just

as enticing as ever as he smirked at her. He was gloating.

"There is no need to eavesdrop when I have impeccable hearing, but I could not have avoided your sweet voice if I tried. The architecture was built to be loud. The walls echo."

*Fucking pain in my ass.*

"Then hear this," she countered, her voice clear as a bell. "You will be *dead* in a minute if you don't shut the fuck up," she nipped as she opened her door and threw her bag in the back seat.

Cassius opened the passenger door and climbed in, grinning devilishly, twisting his fingers along his lips to show he'd zipped it.

*If Bryan isn't fucking dead, I'm going to kill him for this.*

# CHAPTER TEN

"LET ME DRIVE," Cassius pleaded.

"I'm fine, I just need to find a motel or... something... When is the next goddamned exit?" Ava moaned.

"There is no need. Pull over and let me drive. You can rest, and when you wake we will be at our destination."

Ava shot him a scathing glance.

"Was this your plan all along? Tag along until I get tired and then bam!

Vamp chow? I don't think so."

Cassis furrowed his eybrows.

*Is that what she thinks of me?*

*That I'm just waiting for her to let her guard down and I'll finish the claim?*

Her words hurt him, because he could not understand why she would think such things. It had been four years since he'd bitten her, and he'd done everything in his power to prove to her he would not force her hand, despite the fact it would be easier.

Everything would be so much easier if he could complete his claim. If he could make her like he was.

But Cassius would not take such a choice from Ava. He knew all too well how it felt to be born into a life of blood and ash without any say. His words to Leon echoed in his brain.

*My salvation is not worth the price of her choice.*

What more could he do to make her understand that he could never harm her?

"Your words wound me. But it does not change the truth. You *are* tired, and you need rest. My only *plan* is to see to it that we arrive on time, and that you are well rested enough to... how did you say it? Save the day?"

Ava yawned, her jaws stretching like that of a cat in an irrefutable sign that she did indeed need rest.

"Trust me, Ava," Cassius pressed.

Ava sighed, glancing at Cassius for a moment, and he could see she was more than just tired of driving.

She was tired of hiding, too. Hiding behind vicious words and walls erected around her that prevented anyone from seeing the truth. Cassius understood such things. It wasn't as if he hadn't erected walls around himself or his residence. He'd purposefully refrained from telling *anyone* other than Leon that he was leaving the glittering world of the high covens, leaving Eden for good.

He'd hidden in the forest, skirting by on corpse blood for nearly fifty years, passing his endless nights with somber piano music, dry wine, and guilt until he'd followed Taijiri to that frat house.

Until he'd laid eyes on a struggling, dying human with fire in her eyes and a will so very strong it made Cassius drop to his knees that very night and take her hand.

He knew then that nothing else would matter. Nothing else mattered in that moment except her delicate wrist in his hand, the blood in her veins that begged to hold on to dear, dear life.

It was clear to him then, before he even knew her, that she was more than a beautiful college student who had ended up in the wrong place at the wrong time.

Ava was, and continued to be, a fighter, and if the last four years had taught him anything, it was that. And as Cassius looked at Ava's tired eyes, he knew he needed a fighter.

He needed *her,* and she would be the death of him.

"Fine. But if you try anything, and I mean anything..." she nipped as she pulled the car over to the side of the road.

Cassius watched as she threw the car

in park, as her hands gripped the steering wheel. She looked on ahead for a moment before letting her shoulders relax and then, she turned her eyes of fire on him.

Would it ever cease?

The feeling of warmth spreading through his veins, lighting him up and making him feel alive?

He hoped it never would.

"If you try anything I will fucking stake you in this car and I won't be sorry about it. Got it?" Her words were full of bite, but Cassius knew it was an empty threat. After all, she threatened him constantly, and yet here they were, pulled off to the side of the road in the middle of nowhere in the dead of night.

Together.

*That has to count for something right?*

"I promise." Cassius nodded.

Ava sighed as she opened her car door and he did the same. As he rounded the front of the car, meeting her in the middle, she stopped. She looked up at him in the midst of the headlights for a moment. He could feel her pulse racing, the blood rushing beneath his skin like a river. His stomach twisted into knots, and he knew it wasn't due to hunger.

He longed in that moment to reach out to her, run his fingers along her soft, supple skin and tilt her head up until his lips could claim hers, and perhaps then she would understand.

That they were *bonded.*

Not just by blood, but by cirumstance.

By fate.

But Cassius did not reach out and touch her. He did not invade her space or attempt to annihilate the fortress that protected her from the outside world, from him.

Instead, he walked past her, rounding to the driver side without a word, the only sound the purr of the Impala's engine, and Ava's tired sigh.

He'd never driven Ava's car before. In fact, he had not driven a car since the 80's.

There was no need for Cassius to own anything. Paperwork meant there was an evidentiary trail, even if he used one of his aliases, and it was not as if he could not walk, or find other transportation, not to mention Taijiri would not object to him borrowing his Camaro, as long as he was home.

He familiarized himself with her controls, appreciating the simplicity and the mechanics of the 1969 car that Ava called hers. He was not entirely sure how she'd come to own such a beautiful machine, but it suited her nonetheless.

Ava curled up in the passenger seat, tucking her legs to her chest. She wrapped her arms around them, and he noticed she poignantly posed her fists in front of him, one hand gripping a stake, as a display of dominance.

Though it was not needed, he knew it made her feel better and so he did not say anything. Instead, he only pulled the car out on the road.

"Sweet Dreams, Ava."

"Fuck you," she grumbled sleepily, and he had to contain his laugh. Her prickly attitude was both charming and endearing to him, for she was not the first woman in his life who'd had a sharp tongue.

Though the immediate thought pushed images of Eden forth, Cassius combatted them with one look at the pretty slayer in the seat next to him.

*She is nothing like Eden.*

*She has a heart.*

The darkness that blanketed them on all sides was thick, and Cassius hoped they would arrive at their destination soon.

Cassius grabbed her phone on the dashboard, checking the map when a notification came through.

A text.

From an *Asshole.*

Cassius wondered for a moment who Ava would deem so terrible they would not have a name in her contacts.

*You up, Kitten?*

Cassius felt his blood slow. Not only was it an invasion of privacy, but the tone suggested this was someone she knew well. Well enough this *Asshole* had given her a pet name.

Curiosity got the better of him as he looked to his side, noting that Ava was sound asleep. Her fist still curled tightly around the stake, but her mouth had gone slack, and her head lolled to the side. She was, as he would say, out like a light.

Cassius swallowed lightly as he scrolled up her text log, and it did not take him long to realize who *Asshole* was.

Cassius set her phone on the dash once more, as an air of shame and guilt befell him.

His suspicions were in fact, confirmed. Ava and Dallas, it seemed, *did* have a relationship. One they were not public about. His heart ached at this knowledge, and he looked at her once more. He was not angry, nor jealous. He was only numb.

What did Jake Dallas possess that he did not?

Was it because he was... human?

Cassius had his suspicions about Malcolm's partner, ever since TerrorCon. He'd seen the way Jake Dallas looked at Ava in the Dark Hearts Club, felt his anger, the rage from his fist when he'd seen her bleeding on the floor, in his arms of all places.

Together.

Albeit, Cassius had been fighting the

overwhelming desire to sink his teeth into Ava at the time—her blood was on display from her bout with the Incubus who'd bitten her, and Cassius had only acted on instinct with concern for Ava—Dallas's reaction was more than telling. Dallas had feelings for the slayer, too.

Perhaps even *loved* her.

How did Ava feel about him?

Did she love him as well?

Cassius abandoned the thoughts, for they were a dangerous road to take. He'd been down it before, with Eden.

No, he did not need to know such things. Not if he wanted to remain focused on the task at hand, and that was finding their friend.

Ava twitched, drawing his attention. A soft whimper left her throat, and she gripped her stake tighter. Of course, the nightmares that haunted her would not rest just because she was far from home.

Instinctively and without warning, Cassius reached his right hand out, tracing his fingers over her fist—the very one curled around her precious stake. He ran them smoothly over her knuckles, before letting his palm kiss the back of her warm hand, and in that moment Cassius knew.

It would never matter what she did or did not do. It would never matter who she loved or didn't love.

For it would never change the reality of their bond, and it certainly would never change how he felt about her.

And such a realization was more brutal a death than any at the hand of her stake.

Cassius let go of her hand as he

turned the radio up a fraction, letting the soft sounds of Taylor Swift and a man crooning about living forever fill the space. It pulled him back to the here and now, the real reason he'd come on this trip.

To save his friend.

And as Ava's breathing settled to a steady hum and her pulse stilled, that was exactly what Cassius vowed to do.

# CHAPTER ELEVEN

*AVA STOOD IN the darkness, the smell of blood and death pungent in the air. Though everywhere she looked was nothing but shadows, and there was no way out that she could see.*

*"You will never escape," a voice echoed in the darkness.*

*Ava held her arms close, a chill overtaking her. Her feet were cold, covered in thick, wet liquid.*

*Blood.*

*She was standing in a puddle of blood.*

*Ava looked up to the black, starless sky, and she knew the voice was right. Perhaps this was where it ended. Perhaps this was where it was always supposed to end.*

*Ava turned in the darkness, and a trail of slick, wet, shimmering blood stood out to her. So she followed it, like a moth to a flame. One bare foot in front of the other, letting the crimson liquid run over her skin. She did not slip or trip, her gait steady.*

*A figure stood at the edge of the path, illuminated by light. One sole light in the darkness. It called to her, filled her with a warmth and a peace that settled all the demons inside of her.*

*But who was the man silhouetted by the light?*

*An angel?*

*Before she could find out, she was startled.*

*"Ava," another voice called to her from the darkness, and she turned around abruptly. She could see nothing in the vast blackness, but she could feel a presence.*

*"Hello?" she called out, her stomach churning. But no one responded.*

*When she turned around, the light had dimmed, and she had gotten further away.*

*It was so dark, so cold.*

*Ava huffed indignantly as she set forth for the light once more, this time with steadfast feet. She skipped through the pools of blood, picking up into a run.*

*Ava ran and ran as fast as she could, needing to find the light again. Needing its warmth, its awe and wonder.*

*But every step she took, every moment her feet hit the ground beneath her, the light only receded.*

*"No, come back!" she called out, but it was no use.*

*Ava stopped to catch her breath as reality blanketed her like a thick fog.*

*The blood covered her legs and feet, and when she brought her hands up she could see they were stained too.*

*"Come back!" she called out in agony, but all there was, was the scent of fire and ash, of death and blood.*

*There was no response. No voice to call out to her, no light to comfort her. She was well and truly alone, in the darkness. Her mind replayed the death of her parents, of Ross, and the monsters she'd slain like a highlight reel.*

*Blood, fire.*

*Ash.*

*Ava closed her eyes, forcing back tears. She would always be alone, because those closest to her were nothing but cannon fodder. She would always be alone, because she was a monster.*

*A soft, featherlight touch stroked her skin, and her blood warmed on contact. The warmth she sought blossomed throughout her being and she opened her eyes. The light was blinding, and she could not make out a figure.*

*She could only lean into the light, praying that it would dispel the darkness.*

Ava felt a soft touch nudging her. Sleep disintegrated from her as she opened her eyes. Her muscles were cramped and sore, and for a moment she wasn't certain where she was, but it certainly didn't feel like home.

When her vision sharpened as she laid her eyes on the culprit who had awakened her from her slumber, her blood chilled. Cassius sat in the driver seat of her Imapala, looking like a damned oasis in a desert.

"I thought you may be hungry," he said as he nodded to the Stop-N-Go in front of them. Artificial light filled Ava's car, and she glanced at the clock radio. It was near four in the morning.

"Guess I slept a little longer than I wanted..." she grumbled as she wiped her eyes.

Cassius's voice was soft when he spoke as if he was sad. Upset. Which was strange to Ava.

*What the fuck does he have to be upset about?*

As she thought the bitter thought, she remembered the events of yesterday, the very ones that led her to this car, with him.

*Bryan, of course.*

*Way to be insensitive, Ava.*

"Sleep okay?" he asked.

Ava focused on his glowing green emerald eyes, and opened her mouth to respond, but it was as if she was at a loss for words. Something about the way in which Cassius spoke made her feel as if he was asking something else, some question she was not sure how to answer. She shook her head, dispelling the strange thought.

*I am just out of sorts because of that*

*stupid nightmare.*

"Like a baby," she said with a smile as she opened the door.

Cassius remained in the car, and he did not move.

Ava stretched in the crisp, cool air, her Blue Oyster Cult shirt rising up above her navel as she reached above her head for the moon hanging in the sky. She wasted no time heading into the Stop-N-Go, her stomach growling ferociously.

*Good call, Cas.*

Though she would never admit out loud that perhaps stopping for food was a good idea, she was thankful he'd decided to do so.

Ava perused the ready made counter, noting there were at least three other individuals in the store aside from the burly cashier. A side glance told her they were all men, and judging by the sound of their heavy boots and slurred speech, they were on their way home from the bar.

Ava quietly opened the Krispy Kreme Donut case, selecting a jelly filled donut for herself. She closed the donut case and headed over to the self-serve coffee machines, at the same time one of the men seemed to stumble up.

"Why hello there," he said mid-burp.

Ava rolled her eyes, ignoring him.

The man looked to be about six foot at least, stocky but not as muscular as Dallas. Though the scruffy five o clock shadow and the light wrinkle at the corner of his eyes reminded her of him.

"Sweetheart, I'm talking to you," he drawled, and Ava pursed her lips.

It wasn't that she felt threatened or worried at all in this man's presence, but more or less that she'd just woken up, and was not ready to deal with the normal breed of asshole she often found herself dealing with quite yet. She hadn't even had herself a coffee yet.

"Let's get something straight here, dickwad. I aint your sweetheart, and I don't give a fuck if you're talking to me."

One of the other men joined tall, big and stupid, this one a much skinnier version, but dressed in the same grungy digs with the same heavy boots and look of inebriation.

"Woohoo, Earl, seems like you found yourself a biter," he taunted.

*Earl?*

*Really?*

*Could they be more stereotypical?*

Ava finished filling up her cup, and moved to grab another one, if only to show the presence of two cups, which meant she was not alone.

Not that she *needed* Cas's help or anything.

Besides, it was his idea to stop.

As she started to fill the cup with liquid, the third bristly bear joined the party. Ava hurriedly capped off the second coffee, trying to get around them, but it seemed as if they'd boxed her in.

"Excuse me, *Earl*," she nipped, but he blocked her from moving.

"Not until you apologize to Daddy, little brat."

Ava felt her stomach turn. It wasn't as if this piece of work knew anything about her, but the words left her feeling disgusted.

There was truly only one man who could call her a brat and get away with it.

"Look, asshole. It's early, and I'm really not in the fucking mood. Move. The. Fuck. Out of my way."

"Or what, sweetheart?" he asked with a lascivious grin. His cohorts chuckled behind him, and Ava heard the bell on the door jingle.

"Okay, so I guess you're big, and stupid, too. Cool. Wanna play fuck around and find out? Be my guest."

She swung her leg out, applying pressure to just behind Earl's knee. In his drunken state, he went down just as she suspected, like a sack of potatoes, falling on his ass.

Ava stepped around him, just as the cashier was filling up the donut case with more donuts, completely unphased. Although, Ava had to wonder if that meant this was a normal sort of occurrence in these parts or if the cashier was so over their job, they just didn't care.

She scanned the new additions, noting one of them was red velvet supreme. She'd never much cared for the flavor before TerrorCon, but after she'd returned home she'd had a strange craving for it. So, she grabbed a fresh one, tucking it into the bag with her jelly filled donut, the groaning sounds of Earl behind her like music to her ears.

"I'll just take these, when you're ready," she said to the cashier, noting her two coffees and donuts.

Earl's friends helped him up, scoffing.

"Fucking stupid man. Really thought

going to that bitch bar would have gotten me laid, but fuck no…"

Ava's blood stilled.

Bitch bar?

What were they talking about?

Tall, skinny and stupid helped his friend up, answering her thoughts.

"All the bitches up in the Drowned Clam's aint good 'nuff for ya anyway. Maybe we'll have better luck at the Marquis."

Before Ava could process the idiot's words, the cashier rung her up. Ava fished around in her jeans pocket, pulling out a small wad of cash. She never left home without at least forty dollars in cash in her pocket, just in case. After she'd left her wallet in Sam Kingsley's room at TerrorCon, she'd vowed to always keep it on her.

The events of TerrorCon were still blurry to her. She remembered parts of it so vividly, and others she worried were lost forever.

She remembered Sam Kingsley sharing a drink with her, remembered being wrapped up in his arms, how he felt as he filled her. But she also remembered his fangs sinking into her skin, his erection flailing about as she and Dallas exercised the demonic incubus possessing him.

But after that, much was a blur and neither Malcolm nor Dallas seemed to want to talk about it. Bits and pieces surfaced every now and then, of things that didn't make sense, and all Malcolm had offered her was "the anti-venom took awhile to combat the toxin, which can cause hallucinations."

But Hallucinations didn't touch you, or sing to you, and Ava could have sworn she heard someone singing to her, "Don't fear the reaper."

Ava tossed her money on the counter. "So, you, uh... wouldn't know how far the Marquis is from here, would you?" she asked nonchalantly.

The young woman behind the counter sighed.

"That place is nothing but trouble. You don't want any parts of it."

Ava stood straighter.

"Oh really? Why's that?"

"That place is cursed."

"What do you mean cursed?" Ava tucked the donuts underneath her arm.

"Before it was the Marquis, it belonged to a wealthy couple. Lots of murders happened in those walls. Place should be torn down."

Ava grabbed the cups.

"Let's just say… I like a little danger. How far away is it?"

The cashier looked at her cautiously. "About thirty minutes south of here. But it'll be closed until Friday. The new owners have been working on a 'Masquerade' bar or something, sposed' to open up then."

Ava nodded. "I thought it was the Marqius Masquerade and Funhouse?" she asked.

The cashier nodded absentmindedly.

"Place changed owners not that long ago. Some high-brow chic bought it about a year ago. Amara something or other. Guess they wanted to add some luxury to the place."

"Of course. What's more luxurious

than a cursed bar?" she teased.

"Don't say I didn't warn you."

And with that, the bell jingled and another couple of patrons walked in.

"Keep the change," Ava said as she exited the store, only to find Cassius leaning against the hood of the Impala.

Watching her.

Amidst the hazy dusk light, he looked stunning. Like a model on the cover of a rock album or something. His expression was unreadable, as always, though.

Ava leaned on the hood next to him and offered him a coffee.

"Spur of the moment. I don't even know if you drink coffee, since you never show up with one yourself but…"

Cassius looked at the cup like it was made of lava and he would expire if he touched it. She almost pulled it away, but he stopped her. He slid his hand over hers, taking the cup gingerly.

Ava noted the feel of his skin on hers was light, like a feather.

Soft.

Her skin prickled with goosebumps and her blood boiled beneath the surface. Her entire being felt warm. Surely it was not because of his touch. Surely it was due to the warmth emanating from the outside of the flimsy cardboard cup.

"Thank you," he said.

She held out the donut bag.

"I do know you like these, though," she said quietly in response as she held the red velvet donut out to him.

Cassius smiled, showing just a hint of fang.

"Are you sure you do not want it? You

nearly mauled me for it last time."

Ava rolled her eyes.

"Just take the fucking donut. Pain in my ass."

# CHAPTER TWELVE

CASSIUS'S HEART LIFTED at the kind gesture. While rare, these moments fueled his desire more than he cared to admit. He shifted closer to Ava against the hood of the Impala. She pretended not to notice.

When she shifted her weight only a fraction, moving an inch closer to him, he pretended not to notice.

"So, the cashier said the Marquis is

about thirty minutes down the road, but she says it doesn't open until Friday. Something about them adding a Masquerade Bar onto the property." Ava shrugged as she finished her donut, the red jelly staining her lips bright red. The sight flared the beginnings of bloodlust in Cassius's stomach, causing his throat to go dry. He looked away, taking a sip of his coffee, which was much more bitter than he cared for, but it was a welcome distraction. He puckered his lips from the overbearing burnt taste.

"You do drink coffee... right?" she asked, her voice carrying a hint of concern.

"Yes, I do. It is just very... bitter."

"So, you're not one of those 'I drink my coffee as black as my soul' assholes, then."

Cassius let out a small chuckle. "I assure you, I am not," he said as he popped the last bit of donut in his mouth. "But I have had worse."

"Cashier says the place is haunted, too." Ava's lips pulled up into a wicked grin.

"Thinking of doing a bit of recon are you, Detective?"

"I mean, if it's closed, then there won't be anyone else poking around there, will there?" Her eyes sparkled with anticipation.

Cassius picked up his coffee, crumpling the remains of paper from their breakfast. Ava did the same, heading for the driver seat.

The sun would soon be up, and another day laid to rest. Cassius could not help the dread that continued to build in his stomach, worrying that Bryan had already succumbed to an ill fate, and they would be too late. He also worried that maybe they were way off base, and would come up with nothing once they found the Marquis, and that all of it would be some wild goose chase. If only there was a way to know for sure instead of taking a shot in the dark.

But despite knowing the odds may be against them, Cassius stole a glance at the slayer beside him, taking in the sight of her slightly disheveled hair, her fixed gaze of determination, and her jelly-stained lips, and he knew there was no one else he'd rather be in the dark with. A faint stirring in his blood told him perhaps she felt the same, even if she did not say so.

"Stop looking at me like that." Ava

sighed, never taking her eyes off the road.

"Like what?" he said smoothly.

"Like you want to eat me."

Cassius couldn't help but shake his head, turning his gaze to the window.

"I do not wish to *eat* you."

"You lie like a fucking rug. Just remember the deal. Keep your fangs to yourself or I will fucking stake you."

Cassius quietly stared out the window at the passing forests as the sun started to peek through the silhouetted treetops, all amber and ochre, like the light when it caught in Ava's eyes.

"So you say," he murmured as they rounded a long, winding road, in chase of ghosts once more.

# CHAPTER THIRTEEN

AVA TURNED THE car off, but she did not vacate right away. Her heart would not stop racing and she felt as if it would burst right out of her chest. Surely Cassius could hear it thumping away like a drum this closely.

Cassius did not move either, and Ava noted he looked lost in thought as he stared out the window at the Marquis Masquerade and Fun House. The sign itself was ornate, gilded with unlit bulbs, and reminded her of the Las Vegas sign she'd seen in all those travel channel shows she'd binged in college.

She felt a sting of guilt, wondering if she'd been too rude or brash with Cassius, but she knew there was no other choice. She could not afford to get too comfortable with the vampire beside her, no matter how smooth his voice sounded, or how good he smelled, or how enticing he appeared. Falling victim to Cassius was truly a death wish.

*But maybe I like a little danger,* she had told him once.

Was it still true?

She thought it was, but she was certain there were some alleys she did not want to venture down, lest she be met with harsh realities and truths.

The sun was starting to bathe the world in the beginnings of dawn when she decided to turn the idling car off.

Cassius was in no danger of turning to dust.

She had learned some vampires could walk in the daylight without harm, him being one of them. History and lore did not seem to have an answer as to why some had this ability and others did not, but Ava suspected it had to do with age, or perhaps when the vampire was sired or turned. She had no idea how old Cassius was, and though she'd wondered on occasion, she could not bring herself to ask. Fleeting were the moments she wondered about the creature beside her, and when the thoughts came, she quickly diminished them. They would not make a difference in the grand scheme of things. Come hell or high water, one day, she would undoubtedly put a stake through his heart. Though he hadn't made a move to do so yet, she knew the day would come when Cassius would have to give into what he was. He could not fight this bond between them forever, she was sure of it. All the lines converged into one point, all the lore said the very same thing. No bond was meant to be contested, to be ignored.

It was kill or be killed.

He may have saved her life that fated night, but by doing so he also condemned it.

The only choice he had was to either drain her like a juicebox or make her a monster like him, and neither of those options appealed to her. She'd wondered in the depths of her own despair on lonely nights if she would have still clung to the sliver of life he promised her by claiming her blood, had she known then what she knew now, and the fact she could not answer herself caused her a great deal of turmoil regarding the matter.

Cassius moved to open the door, and Ava followed suit, banishing all stray sugar-induced thoughts and daydreams of the golden haired vampire from her mind. She had bigger things to worry about.

Set against a rather scenic landscape, the Marquis was not as opulent as its name or signage would suggest. While one would expect ivory pillars and Grecian grandeur, the Marquis itself looked more like a weathered plantation, left alone on the edge of the forest to fade into the shadows with time.

"Well, it's definitely got the 'someone was murdered here' vibe," Ava said as she bent over slightly, sliding out the stake she kept between her jeans and the inside of her boot.

Cassius's gaze dipped to the sliver of wood that could end him at any moment.

Ava stole a glance, noting that doing so made her blood heat like molten lava. One day she would not feel such things, and she had to remember that. She had to remember what she was fighting for.

*A chance to live.*

"It is hard to believe this is where your darkest desires are brought to life," he drawled, his tone laced with judgmental apprehension.

"What's the matter, Cas? Does the haunted mansion scare you?" she teased him as she quickened her pace, strolling to the front doors.

Cassius shook his head. "The only thing that scares me, my sweet Avarice, is that we may be too late."

His words sobered her. He was right to worry. There was a sliver of a chance they'd be too late. Find Bryan chopped to bits or left for dead in this very building, but she refused to fall into such awful thoughts. She had also been left for dead once, and here she stood. No, she had to have *hope.*

Hope that Bryan was somehow here, alive and waiting for them.

Ava walked up the steps, the stairs creaking and groaning in her wake.

The windows were fogged, strewn

with fresh cobwebs in the corners, and she could barely make out anything inside.

"I'll take the right, you take the left," she commanded, not giving Cassius much time to answer as she headed back down the steps, rounding about to the right.

"Of course," he agreed, and Ava noted his voice sounded off. As if he was not entirely focused on the matter at hand; as if he was distracted.

Ava held her stake close to her chest as she crept quietly around the wrap-around porch. The parking lot had been stark empty upon arrival as she expected, but she could not shake the feeling like she was being preyed upon.

Stalked, watched.

By something *other* than an annoying

vampire who looked good in leather pants.

She slid her back up against the faded paneling, catching her breath as a rat skittered across the floorboards, nearly making her jump. Clearly, whoever had purchased the place did not care to upgrade the outside as much as the inside.

"Fucking rat," she huffed out breathlessly, feeling both on edge and embarrassed.

She continued slowly creeping around the porch. No windows existed on the side of the house, and she found that quite odd. While the house looked ancient enough, she was fairly certain even old colonials had windows on the main floor, but the only ones she'd seen were those in the front of the house, flanking both sides of the door.

And just as she quickly turned the corner, a heavy force slammed her back against the wall and she nearly dropped her stake, being caught off guard,

"What the hell? Ava? What are you doing here?" the familiar dark, deep voice caused Ava's heart to race and her blood to heat, although it had nothing to do with vampirism.

Ava held her stake against a solid, defined chest, pressing the sharp tip in just enough she truly could draw blood if she desired.

But that was the thing about being trapped in Dallas's large, solid arms, backed against a wall.

She didn't *want* to escape, and she hated how his dominant nature brought out the parts of her she hated the most.

The weak, needy, submissive part of her that longed to be held, to be worshipped, and to be *loved.*

But Ava did not love Jake Dallas. No. What they had was far from love.

"Put me the fuck down, asshole." She twisted in his grip, driving the tip of her stake into his chest only a bit to prove she wasn't in the mood to play games right now.

*What the hell is he doing here?*

Dallas grabbed the edge of her stake and with one pull, he had it out of her hands, despite her tight grip. Ava whimpered in defeat, scowling in protest.

"Not until you tell me what the hell you're doing in this hellhole."

Dallas pressed his chest against hers, which wasn't a hard feat, considering he was built like a brick house. The man had more muscles than was probably necessary, but that was due to an extensive work out regimen that Ava had assumed had more to do with working out stress than staying in shape, though she couldn't be sure. It wasn't like she and Dallas talked much when they were together, especially outside of hunting. When they were alone, there was hardly any time *to* talk, being as most of their interests were centered around training and...

"Hey, D, look what the fucking cat dragged in. Ava's gonna have a conniption when..."

Malcolm shoved Cassius forward, and Ava's eyes widened in surprise. She looked between Cassius—who didn't look too offended by the gesture, only annoyed—back to Dallas who still had her pressed against the wall. She noted the flicker of something in Cassius's gorgeous green eyes; something she couldn't quite place. But it looked like pain. Disappointment, even.

"I can explain," she said, looking back at Mal and Cassius.

Cassius crossed his arms, drawing back his lips to reveal pointed fangs, visibly *hissing* at Dallas.

"Put her down, you big brute. She is not the enemy. *We* are not your enemy."

Mal snapped. "You don't fucking call the shots here, tick." He pointed his own stake at Cassius, inches from his chest.

Dallas growled, but he moved back enough to give Ava some space.

Suddenly, her cheeks felt flushed and her thighs became slick and wet.

*Now is not the time!*

"Just calm your fucking tits, Mal. I said I can explain," she said as she pushed Dallas in the chest. He faltered only a bit, a murderous look in his eyes she'd never quite seen out of the boxing ring or the bedroom.

"Then start talking," Mal bit.

"We don't have time for this," Cassius growled as he laced his fingers around Mal's stake. He pulled it away, and the sound of cracked wood was most prevalent in the air.

Ava's stomach twisted as she realized he'd *snapped* the wooden stake in half. With his hand.

*All the more reason to remember your end game.*

"We have a... mutual contact," Ava started.

Cassius's gaze focused on Ava, his

lips tightening.

"A friend. He... he needs our help. I think he was kidnapped."

"Isn't that a job for the police?" Dallas asked, crossing his arms. He took a step closer to Ava, still giving her space but letting her know he was not done with her, by far.

"He was on one of those singles sites, and this chick messaged him about meeting up and coming here." Ava motioned to the empty building.

"And you didn't tell the police?" Mal said as he regarded Cassius.

"No. Because I firmly believe that whoever is responsible for taking my friend, isn't your run of the mill hot goth babe."

"What makes you say that?" Mal asked skeptically.

Ava growled as she stomped her foot in annoyance. "Call it a fucking hunch! I just know, okay!"

"What are you psychic now, too?" Dallas quipped.

Ava glared at him. "You never questioned my judgment, before."

"That was before I found you sneaking around a Djinn nest with a fucking vampire."

"Djinn?" Ava asked, feeling her temperature rise. How dare Dallas insinuate such things.

*Who the hell does he think he is?*

"Yeah. We got reports about some locals who claimed to have escaped, thought it might be vamps, came down from Michigan to check it out. Turns out..."

"Vamps aren't the only invasive

species in town," Dallas growled.

"Just you two? Where's the rest of the Scooby Gang?" Ava asked, crossing her arms.

Hunter and Tito are following up with Vinny on a lead about..." Mal's gaze quickly flashed to Cassius, and Ava understood.

The lack of words told her all she needed to know. She'd never been forthcoming with the vampire in her presence about her endeavors to try and lift his blood claim, and she didn't have any intention of doing so right at this very pivotal moment in time.

"Djinn are usually more isolated," Cassius said smoothly, pulling her attention once more.

"Got something you want to share with the class, Cas?" she bit out at the same time Dallas spoke, effectively canceling out her speech.

"You think we're fucking lying?" Dallas's shoulders tensed as he took a step toward Cassius.

"I said no such thing. Just making an observation." Cassius's voice was like velvet, tinged with a venomous bite Ava had never heard before, but she could not deny the sound stirred something within her.

Something she did not wish to acknowledge even in the dead of night, alone.

"There's also been reports of a vampire coven in the area for some time, but they didn't seem to settle until recently. That's the problem with hunting, too many ticks, not enough of us to go around and put them in their place," Mal said as he slid the pad of his fingertip over the sharp, broken point of his stake. His eyes met Cassius's, both of them staring at one another like a Mexican standoff.

"Two birds one stone. I understand," Cassius said, his voice falling back to normal.

"To answer your question, Ava. Yes, I know of the Djinn. Their kind have been around since the dawn of vampires, but we are not... allies. The Djinn operate similar to that of the demons, the Incubi. Like us, they need human blood—" His words hung in the air for a moment, leaving Ava feeling rather nervous. His eyes met hers for a moment and it seemed as if he regretted saying such things. Which would be insane.

"They need human blood, but not for

the same reason we do. It does not fulfill them. What they seek is the essence, the desire. The *hope*. Djinn pray on wishes."

"Or your darkest desires," Ava mumbled, remembering Enchantress's message to Bryan.

*Where your darkest desires come to life.*

"Maybe we should work together," Mal said cautiously.

"Are you fucking crazy?" Dallas growled at the same time Ava chimed in with "Absolutely not"."

Mal looked everyone over before settling his gaze on his sister, raising an eyebrow.

"If your friend *is* in custody of the Djinn or the vampires, you'll probably need backup anyway. Unless, of course, you've killed a Djinn before," Mal snarked as he pulled out his cell phone. He looked at the glowing device, tapping out a text, though Ava wasn't certain to who.

Cassius looked as if he wanted to speak, but he thought better of it.

Ava's gaze flickered from one man to the next, all standing before her as her brother's words sunk in. He was right. She hadn't thought there would be any other threat, outside of vampires. She'd never faced down a Djinn before, and though it seemed Cassius *knew* what they were, she wasn't entirely sure she could trust him, though she wanted to.

A part of her buried deep beneath the surface *begged* her to trust him. He hadn't hurt her yet. In fact, he'd come in handy and aided her on more than one occasion.

But was it enough?

Faced with a monster she knew nothing about, could she put her life in the hands of another monster?

*A monster who saved your life once before...*

"Fine," Ava answered, not missing Dallas's cursing behind her.

"Wise choice, Simba," Mal said as he looked at Cassius with a smirk.

"In that case," Mal cleared his throat as he slid his phone back into his back pocket. "Cas, you come with me. Dallas, take Ava back to base and get her up to speed, and give Vinny a call. If anyone can find some blueprints on this place, it'll be him."

"Where the hell do you think you're going?" Ava nipped.

Cassius sank his hands into his

pockets, sending her a reassuring look.

"Hunting of course," Mal smiled wickedly.

A hurricane of concern fluttered in her stomach, though she could not discern who she was more concerned about—her brother, or the monster accompanying him.

# CHAPTER FOURTEEN

CASSIUS FOLLOWED MALCOLM around the back of the building toward the woods. In any other scenario, he would have been more cautious of the man, but with Ava near, he knew he was safe. For the moment, anyway.

"I have to give you credit, Cas. You have more balls than I thought you did."

"Excuse me?" Cassius responded, taken off guard.

Malcolm stepped down from the porch, looking up at Cassius, who stood still as a stone.

"It's been what, four years since you marked my sister?" Mal pulled out a package of cigarettes from his back pocket and Cassius pursed his lips.

"I can assure you, it is not what it looks like."

"What was your plan?" Mal lit his cigarette, and Cassius wrinkled his nose at the smell of smoke. He'd never cared for it.

"Make up some little story about a rescue, sequester my sister on a road trip to the middle of nowhere, and BAM!" Mal clapped his hands, loud enough it stirred the birds in the nearby trees.

"Believe me or not, I have never lied to you once, Malcolm. Our friend is in danger, and we are wasting time."

"How do I know you didn't pluck the poor bastard off yourself? All part of your devious little plan to get Ava to trust you."

"You are implying she trusts me at all," Cassius bit as Mal blew smoke in the air.

Malcolm turned with a nod as he headed for the woods.

"Well, I don't. Trust you, that is. Not as far as I can fucking throw you."

"So why ask for my help?" Cassius kept his distance if only to avoid the putrid smoke.

"Keep your friends close, but your enemies closer."

"I am not your enemy, Malcolm. I never have been." Cassius sighed as he followed him into the woods. Just a hair into the woods, he could see two motorcycles parked just behind a large bush next to an old cellar door in the ground. Of course, that was why they hadn't seen them. Cassius stood still as Malcolm threw his leg over the seat.

"I take it you were not able to break the lock?" Cassius nodded to the doors.

"It's old, rusted. Probably locked from the inside. Dallas and I were looking for a way in, scouting the area until..."

"And now what? You've abandoned your search on account of me? I'm flattered, Malcolm, really but—"

Malcolm nodded to the larger cycle, which boasted painted flames. It was a large bike, bigger than anything Cassius had seen in a good while.

"You know how to drive one of these things?" Mal said, taking another drag of his cigarette.

Cassius shrugged. "I have never cared for motorcycles."

"So that's a no, then." Mal cracked his neck.

Cassius felt rather agitated. "I only said I did not care for them. Not that I don't have experience." He stared at the beautiful chrome, the shimmering paint, and his stomach growled with hunger. He closed his eyes as he realized with a wave of nausea that it had been longer than twenty four hours since he'd fed on the stolen blood from the Willowcrest Morgue. As if perfectly on cue, his throat constricted, feeling dry and desperate. His senses kicked into gear, and he was all too aware of the pain in the ass hunter snickering behind him, egging him on like some town bully.

If only he'd possessed a shred of Eden's heartlessness, he could eliminate Malcolm Crowley and all his interference. It would make things so much simpler, but alas, Cassius could not find it within himself to be so callous toward humans, no matter how annoying one of them may be.

"Then quit pussyfooting around, and let's go," Mal bit as he tossed Cassius the keys and started up his motorcycle.

Cassius caught them in midair, his reflexes much more heightened than the average human's due to his vampirism. He ran his free hand along Dallas's bike, finding himself wondering if Ava had ever been on it. Thoughts of her legs hugging the side of Dallas's hips shot a fire through him, and he knew he should dispel such thoughts, push them down deep into the caverns of his soul.

Cassius threw his leg over the seat, and he had to admit, sitting behind the bars of such a sleek, well kept machine made him feel a sense of power he thought he'd lost long ago. And when the engine roared to life, for a moment, Cassius felt alive in a way he'd never felt in all his years.

***

"It is a bar," Cassius drawled. "And it is ten o'clock in the morning."

"I have it on pretty good authority that it is five o clock somewhere. This is where the Djinn have been spotted. It's also rumored this is where the coven operates out of."

"A hotspot, then," Cassius murmured.

"A literal den of fucking monsters," Malcolm retorted.

Cassius stared at the Drowned Clam, which looked just as run down as the Marquis, and every other building in the town of Albright, Ohio.

"You pulled me from a rescue mission to drag me to a bar—a hotspot—you *think* is full of immortals."

"Are you slow? Have all the years of daywalking rotted your feeble tick brain?" Mal snickered.

"I do not see the point in your actions," Cassius said, dismounting the motorcycle. It was nearing a quarter after ten, and Cassius was starting to feel rather antsy. For such an early hour, the bar itself looked to be quite busy. A pair of women giggled as they walked past him, one of them stealing a glance at him that he could only describe as tempting. He had to admit with her long, dark hair and excited eyes, she was rather attractive.

The blood that flushed her cheeks as she took in the sight of him stirred his hunger, the stolen pulse beneath his skin next to non-existent. His pulse was faint, and he longed for what was out of his grasp. Even the sight of a beautiful woman as it were, was not enough to make his heart race or his black blood rush beneath the surface, and he was certain no one else would ever again. Not now that he'd claimed the sweetest blood for himself.

Wherever Dallas had taken Ava, it was far from his reach, and he was equal parts grateful and angry, but also very hungry.

He forced himself to look away.

"What's the matter, Cas? Feeling a little under the weather?" Malcolm said with mock concern.

"Let us get whatever it is you intend to do, over with. A man's life depends on it."

Malcolm dismounted his bike, heading for the doors with Cassius right behind him.

The inside of the Drowned Clam lived up to its name. The walls were a dark, aged mahogany that reminded Cassius of another place, in another life. It reminded him of Penny's tavern in Portofino.

It reminded him of home.

Cassius had called many places home since those years. Paris, Rome, Ansley. Chester. But nothing had ever truly felt like home, not in the way Portofino did. Even now he missed its salty breezes and the warmth of the tavern when the air turned to a chill.

The man tending the bar was a burly man, with a pointed beard that hung just above where Cassius would assume his navel to be, given the portly shape of the man.

Malcolm pulled up a spot at the bar, not bothering to wait for Cassius. "Two whiskeys, please," he said arrogantly.

Cassius raised an eyebrow at him. "I do not drink whiskey."

Mal chuckled as the bartender set to pouring. "Bold of you to assume it was for you."

Cassius huffed indignantly as the bartender shoved the glass toward Malcolm.

"And for you, Sunshine?" he grumbled.

Cassius's lips twitched, the scent of sweat and liquor clinging to the man was making his stomach flip. His throat was dry, and he knew nothing in the Drowned Clam would clench his thirst.

And then he saw *her.*

Long, silken black hair sprawled down her back, and her vibrant blue eyes sparkled in the light amidst her porcelain skin.

*Enchantress.*

Cassius shook his head, feeling a strange sense of deja vu. She reminded him of someone else. Someone he longed to forget.

It seemed the ghost of Eden Boracelli would haunt him wherever he went.

"Excuse me, Malcolm," he said as he

strode over to the other side of the bar, not giving a care to the annoying Crowley behind him sputtering some nonsense.

Cassius sauntered toward the woman who'd messaged Bryan, his blood running colder than usual due to his lack of sustenance. She sat in a corner booth with two other women who looked like carbon copies of her, albeit with varying facial features. But they were all dressed in black, with the same onyx hair and fair skin. How hadn't he seen it before, he wondered. Though one could argue that photographs on the internet did not do the siren Djinn justice, and perhaps it had been too long since he'd seen one in person. Centuries, even.

The same pair of women who'd passed him on the way in sat at a booth not far away, and he could feel their gaze on him as he walked on by. The air was thick with the perfume of the Djinn, a mix between woodsy citrus and spice. He had to admit it smelled *divine* and stirred a wishful sort of lust in him that was hard to ignore, but that was par for the course for the beautiful creatures. They fed on blood and desire, after all, albeit their desire was less sexual and more to do with hopes and dreams. Cassius had to remember to stay focused. If he wasn't careful, one could fall into the fantasy far too easily and end up deceased, even a monster such as him.

"Can I help you?" The raven-haired kidnapper said as she appraised Cassius with judgmental blue irises.

Cassius hated how easy it was for

him to flip his switch. He mourned the time he was naive, trusting, ignorant to the wills and charms that were pure instinct for a vampire, once they'd learned how to use them.

"You look oddly familiar to me," he said, dropping his voice low enough that bystanders could not hear him. A low hiss echoed near him as Enchantress licked her lips.

She did not betray much. She only smiled softly with a shrug as she roved her gaze over him.

"I've been told I have a… familiar face." Her voice was smooth, but it carried the hint of an accent. Coupled with her deep tone, it was almost hypnotizing.

The two girls in the booth next to them appraised him as well as he stood there, and Cassius noted they looked... *hungry.*

Had Malcolm not said there were reports of deaths?

He wondered how many innocent lives these venomous snakes had caught in their coils, and how long it had been since their last meal. He made a mental note to ask Malcolm about the reports later. After all, if they were to work together, it would certainly be helpful to know the full story.

"Well, perhaps I shall jog your memory." He shifted his stance, loosening his shoulders as he leaned his head to the side. The woman known as Enchantress twisted her lips in thought before responding.

"A face like yours would be hard to forget, but it has been a long week."

Cassius stepped forward, his thrall testing the waters and begging to be free. He hated to use such things, but as Eden had once taught him, power was only as strong as the man who wields it. Though he did not favor using his vampire abilities on other creatures as it often required more strength and energy, and unless one was full and sated, it could be quite draining.

He reached out, feeling the edges of Enchantress's natural aura.

She smiled wickedly as she took a step closer.

"Well this is a surprise. I don't often snag vampires in my nets, but for you I may make an exception." Her eyes glistened as her aura glowed, pulling him in by his thrall, practically

Before Cassius could answer, another

voice stopped him dead in his tracks.

*"Tous les pécheurs seraient misérables au ciel."* The saccharine voice was ghostly, stirring up memories he thought he had long buried. He spun around, taking in the sight of a petite woman, dressed in a pale pink sweater that was rather tight on her small frame. White heart buttons pulled from the overabundance of fair, bountiful cleavage, accented by long, pale blonde curls falling over her shoulders, framing her breasts. Her bright, blood-red lips and dark makeup made her look young—perhaps early twenties—but Cassius knew she was much, much older than that.

*"Elle brûlait trop fort pour ce monde."* Cassius spoke the words as if he'd gone back in time, and perhaps in a way he

had.

"Cassius, what a lovely surprise," she said as she slowly approached him, reaching out to hug him in a polite gesture. Enchantress scoffed, her demeanor shifting from the surprise appearance of the queen in her presence. Though when Amora Medici embraced Cassius, planting a kiss on his cheek, he could not deny the memories as they came flooding back to him.

*"This is madness, Amora, I can not..."* Cassius's heart raced as he tried to catch his breath. She smelled like blood and strawberries mixed with fresh-pressed linen. The scent of blood and sex was prominent, and he was starving.*

*Amora traced her long, pale fingernails along his jaw, tugging his face toward her.*

*"Why not? Do not tell me this is because of... Eden." The way in which she spoke of his betrothed was bitter, spiteful. Though Cassius knew Amora had more than one reason to harbor such hatred for Eden.*

*"I am betrothed to her, Amora. And you are tied to Marcellus." Cassius softly plucked her hand from his face, holding her delicate wrist in his hand, his thumb brushing the underside of her wrist.*

*"Marcellus is my consort, not my mate. We are not as bound as you think."*

*"He is my friend, and I—"*

*"Do you think I don't know what he does? I am a queen, Cassius, there is not much that goes on under my nose that I am not aware of."*

*Cassius turned away, dropping her wrist.*

*"Marcellus loves you, even if he does not show it," Cassius said in defense. Though he knew better than anyone that love was complicated. Marcellus was not unlike his father; raised in blood, wanting for nothing. The world lay at their feet and they were encouraged to partake in all its riches, for that was the mark of a powerful man.*

*"Love does not factor into the equation, Cassius. Our marriage is not so different from yours, you know. The only difference is I have given this coven an heir. I have fulfilled my duty," she bit.*

*"How can you say love is not part of the equation? How can you stand there and preach such things to me, when you are begging for my love?" Cassius exclaimed, feeling hot remorse and guilt mingling with his desire.*

*A part of him longed for love, and he thought perhaps one day Eden would grow into their arrangement, perhaps one day their lovemaking would not feel so empty or one-sided. Perhaps one day, he would be enough. Children or no children, as long as they were together his family could be safe.*

*"You deserve more, dear. You deserve a queen."*

*The party could be heard still, the sound of strings and laughter echoing in the halls of the Medici estate.*

*"That may be so, but I am a man of honor, Amora. I would not put you, or him... or Eden in such predicaments."*

*"What would it take, Cassius? Name your price."*

*Cassius closed his eyes and breathed deep. The scent of fresh blood was so tempting. His cock strained in his pants, knowing the satisfaction the crimson nectar would bring inevitably.*

*But he was stronger than this.*

*Wasn't he?*

*"My heart is not for sale, Amora," he said sternly. "And neither is my bed."*

*"She will never love you, Cassius. Mark my words. Eden is not capable of love for anyone or anything other than her own selfish needs."*

*Cassius shook his head as he headed for the door.*

"Friend of yours, Ami?" Enchantress's tone had shifted to pure intrigue, and Cassius felt a sting of panic. He'd been hiding for so long… the only person who truly knew of his presence, of his whereabouts was Leon.

Would Amora expose him?

Though their affair was brief, he hadn't said goodbye...

Amora pulled back, flashing her bright eyes to Enchantress before speaking.

*Ami?*

*Is that what she goes by now...*

"Ah yes, a friend who I have missed," Amora said sweetly as she tucked her hand underneath Cassius's arm, pulling him away.

# CHAPTER FIFTEEN

"SO, THIS IS why you were avoiding my calls," Dallas grumbled as Ava walked with determination toward the Impala.

"I'm not doing this with you," she bit, feeling a flurry of emotion. She hadn't expected to run into her brother or Dallas. She knew they were on a case, in Ohio, but they could have been good and gone for all she knew. It wasn't like either of them kept her apprised of their plans on a day to day basis.

They were grown men with agendas of their own to service, just as she was a grown woman with her own ghosts to chase.

She didn't owe either of them, especially Dallas, any explanation for... well, anything.

Besides, it wasn't like they were a couple, but the way Dallas was lumbering after her, seething with anger, it felt like maybe...

"Oh no? But you'll creep around with fucking monsters, won't you?"

Ava stopped, dragging her keys out as she came to the car. She reached for the door, but a large, solid hand smacked the side of the door, making her jump. She looked up at Dallas, who was practically fuming.

"And so what if I am? What's it to you? I'm not some Susie fucking homemaker waiting for you to grace me with your calls, Jake. I'm capable of chasing leads and putting said fucking monsters in the ground myself, and I don't need permission form you to do any of it," she bit.

"I never said—" Dallas huffed in frustration.

"Get. Out of my way, Dallas." Ava could feel her temperature flaring. A part of her wanted to take the bait, rise to the fight. She loved to fight, especially if it would undoubtedly end in Dallas putting her in her place—consensually of course—but there was also a part of her that knew at the moment such things would likely be trouble... more trouble than it was worth. Trouble was practically her middle name, after all, she was a Crowley. A death wish was genetic.

Dallas only pursed his lips, nostrils flaring as he looked at her, his eyes alight with something she had seen only a few times before.

*Jealousy.*

*Was he jealous of Cassius?*

The thought was absurd to her.

Why would he be jealous of a vampire?

"I don't think so, Kitten. I'm driving," he said as he shoved her back against the side of the car, the door handle just out of reach. He loomed over her like a much hotter version of The Hulk, the little vein in his neck standing out. Fury looked good on him, but it also stirred feelings within Ava that she despised.

Fear, anxiety, powerlessness.

She'd been training with Dallas for years to break through such barriers, but here she stood, frozen as he pressed his solid frame against her, staring her down with wordless command like the hurricane he was.

At that moment, something in her awakened, rising like a phoenix from the ashes.

Ava's eyebrows furrowed.

"The hell you are, this is my car!" she said as she pushed him aside.

"Why do you insist of being so defiant of everything I say and do?" he growled in response.

Ava opened the door, slamming it into his midsection if only to convey she was not in the mood for his bullshit. He had the audacity to grab his groin and hip, hissing in pain as if her outburst should make her feel any sense of remorse. But it didn't. In fact, Ava wished she had hit him a little harder, turned the tables of punishment on him for a change.

"I don't have time for this. Get in or stay here, I don't give a shit."

She closed the door, but Dallas was in the passenger seat faster than she could start the car and drive off.

"You don't even know where base *is*."

"Then by all means, do something useful and tell me instead of being a jealous dick." The words escaped her mouth, and she almost regretted them.

Almost.

"I'm not jealous of a fucking tick. I'm concerned. About *you*."

"Thanks, but I'm a big girl, Dallas. Or have you forgotten that?" she nipped as she pulled out on the road.

Dallas looked as if he wanted to respond, but thought better of it.

"This conversation isn't over, but right now we have bigger things to worry about. Take route 30 north."

***

Ava pulled into the driveway of what looked to be the most perfect house she'd ever seen. The residential area looked like something out of a movie. Idyllic, even. Dogwood trees flanked the sides of the road along sidewalks, their blooms starting to peak. The sun shone down on the blue house with white trim, and Ava had to do a double take.

*This is base?*

She'd known her brother and the rest of the Goon Squad to take up in motels most of the time when they were on the road, but she also knew they had other secret hideouts like the Bat Cave where they could train, or keep a stash of weapons. Just in case.

Though the idea of anyone training in a house with a white swing on the porch and pale blue shutters made her slightly uncomfortable.

It reminded her of home, as a stray memory pushed forth.

*Ava ran up the steps, nearly missing her mother sitting on the porch swing.*

*"It's eleven thirty." Her mother's voice sounded in her ears. Ava turned on her heel, the leather of her cheerleading shoe squeaking against the wood.*

*"I lost track of time," she lied.*

*Lenora puffed on her cigarette, blowing smoke into the air.*

"Nice try, baby, but I wasn't born last night."

"Mom…"

"I'm not mad, Ava. Just disappointed." Somehow the words made Ava feel worse than if her mother would have been angry. If she would have grounded her on the spot.

"You just don't like Jeremy." She crossed her arms.

"Jeremy is an idiot," her mother said, like it was common knowledge. "And he doesn't respect you. A boy worth your time will respect you."

"Why are you trying to ruin my life?" she grumbled.

Her mother raised an eyebrow. "Oh, Ava. Baby. This isn't ruin. Far from it." She took another drag of her cigarette, pushing herself on the swing. The rusty *metal springs squeaked from the movement.*

*"Whatever. I'm going to bed."*

Ava pushed the memory away, feeling the threat of tears. She didn't think of her mother often. She thought she'd buried all the hurt and pain of her death deep down inside of her, but every once in a while, it would creep back up and grab her by the throat.

"What the fuck is this place?" Ava asked as she turned the car off.

Dallas opened the door, his inflection full of venom.

"Base."

"It looks like a fucking bed and breakfast. You sure you and my brother aren't on a honeymoon or some shit?" she asked as she opened the door, watching Dallas circle around to the front. The sunlight shone on his tan skin, his tousled dark hair, which he'd neglected to cut, against his skin, his almost six-o-clock shadow. He looked rather out of place in such a cozy neighborhood.

He didn't answer her. He only hurried up the white wooden steps and she followed, reluctantly.

Whatever it was they had to do, she wished it to be over as soon as possible so she could get back to the task at hand.

*Finding Bryan.*

Her thoughts wandered for a moment, to her brother and Cassius.

Where were they and why did Mal need him all of a sudden?

What did he have planned?

Dallas lifted up the mat in front of the

door, pulling out a key.

Ava crossed her arms, listening to the sound of the birds chirping. The white swing swung from the light breeze, but the metal didn't squeak.

Dallas opened the door, glaring at her.

"Ladies first."

Ava brushed past him with a huff and into the house. It didn't look as she had expected, in fact it looked quite bare, minimalistic. She slowly walked into the foyer, and Dallas came up behind her after shutting the door. He set the key in a ceramic bowl on the end table in the center, making her jump.

"Welcome to my house," he growled as he stomped toward the kitchen.

The words hit Ava in the chest like a brick.

*His house?*

Dallas never mentioned having a house of his own. As far as she knew, his home was the open road, like her brother, or the rest of the hunters. Then again, there wasn't much about Dallas's past that was open for discussion, if she wanted to discuss it at all. She'd known the man since she was fifteen, well before they'd ever formed a mutual friendship over monster hunting. Dallas did not dwell on the past. He only focused on the present, but she had always been curious.

Every one of them, including her brother, had come to the dark side to hunt vampires and other creatures of the night because, like her, they'd been exposed to the world in the shadows. But even after several years with the

Goon Squad, no one seemed keen on bringing up such ghosts. Instead, they chose to avenge them with every stab and every match.

Ava stood stone cold for a moment as she watched Dallas head for the kitchen, opening the refrigerator. She tried to match up the cottage aesthetic with the motorcycle riding, tattooed man in front of her but she could not see it. Surely, he was joking, or he'd hired one hell of an interior designer.

Nonetheless, she made her way to the kitchen.

Dallas poured himself a drink. A whiskey it looked like. He took a long pull before grabbing her a glass as well.

"This is what's going to happen, Ava. You're going to tell me the truth. And then, I'm going to fill you in on our investigation, and if you listen to me, you can stay and help us."

"How very noble of you to offer me such a deal," she bit, grabbing her drink and nearly downing it. "Maybe you've gotten knocked around a bit too much or that senility is finally kicking in, but last I remember, you don't tell me what the fuck to do."

Dallas glared at her with fire in his eyes.

"I called you. Texted you. You didn't respond, and I thought maybe you were in trouble."

Ava scoffed as she took another drink. "Typical fucking man."

"I'm serious, Ava. You've been avoiding me, ever since..." His voice disappeared into the air, but she knew what he meant. What he wasn't saying.

The last time they'd seen each other things had gotten... blurry.

They were both so very frustrated, stealing moments away on the case they were working together with the rest of the crew.

Training with Dallas had always been a surefire way to blow off steam, to re-circuit herself back to neutral.

But that night... something changed. When Dallas held her down, as he had so many times before, begging her to fight him, Ava's demons rose to the surface.

She'd always attributed the painful memories of powerlessness as part of her process when facing down vamps. Remembering that night she'd almost died, her legs dead weight as they bled out on the concrete floor. The feeling of thrall she'd experienced time and time again from her exposure as vampire bait was hard to combat, but her brother had taught her that the most difficult, painful memories could be a powerful weapon.

But pinned underneath Dallas at that moment, she wanted to give up.

She didn't want to fight Jake Dallas anymore. She wanted to submit, but that was not who she was.

Was Dallas changing her?

When did that happen?

And when he had *held* her in his arms after her momentary lapse of self, she felt a sting of guilt.

Panic.

"Not everything is about you, Dallas," she said, her voice carrying in the small space. "I don't need you to take care of me. I can take care of myself," she bit. "I was trying to save a man from the pitfalls of online dating!"

"With the fucking vampire who bit you!" he roared.

It's not like that! God, you are such a..." she yelled back.

Dallas balled his fist, slamming it against the other side of the refrigerator as he pulled out the bottle of whiskey, pouring another round.

"An asshole? For giving a shit about your safety? Well, excuse me for wanting to protect you."

"Really, Jake? You want to 'protect' me all of a sudden? When the last two years you've done nothing but teach me how to protect myself against vicious monsters? I'm not some fucking damsel and you know that! I don't *need* you or your 'protection'. And besides, if Cas is with me... he isn't killing anyone, and that's a win in my book."

"I'm going to give you to the count of three, Kitten. To. Tell. Me. The. Truth." Dallas's eyes were full of fury, his voice solid and unwavering.

Coupled with his hunched shoulders, and the grip he had on his glass, Ava could not deny he looked quite menacing. When he slowly stalked his way over to her, she found it hard to move. Ava looked up at his bright blue eyes, feeling emboldened as ever, as if she was staring down a scary monster come to drag her to hell. And in a way, that was what Dallas was to her. A monster of her own making. Something she needed to conquer in order to move on with her life. He certainly wasn't anything... more. But even as she tried to convince herself, she knew it was a lie.

When had things gotten so complicated?

"Are you in love with him?" Dallas asked seriously.

Ava's eyes widened in surprise as his words hit her. Surprise gave way to anger, to panic. Her blood ran cold.

"Absolutely not! Are you fucking insane?" she yelled, feeling defensive.

How could he insinuate such a thing?

Didn't he know she loathed the leather-clad vampire for what he had done to her?

Did he not know her at all?

Dallas looked down at her with fire behind his eyes and reached his hand out, grabbing her by the neck. His thumb slid over her jaw, and his grip was stern, fierce.

"Are you in love with me?" His voice was barely a whisper.

Ava could not tear her gaze away from him. Her heart pounded in her chest, and the air felt as if it had been sucked out of the room.

Instinctively, she reached out to push him away, to tell him to fuck right off with his emotional, manipulative words. But instead, her arms slid around his neck, her fingers teasing the edges of his hair. This was familiar, the pain, the force. His hand around her throat.

But what wasn't familiar was the fact she could not bring herself to say 'no.'

So Ava said nothing.

Instead, she leaned up and kissed Jake Dallas with anger, with fury, and guilt.

And when he kissed her back, sliding his tongue into her mouth, she could not resist.

She pulled him closer, seeking the feeling of numbness Dallas always brought her.

Lines blurred when he grabbed her by the hips and lifted her up onto the counter. Glasses skittered across the surface as lust overtook them both.

Ava tugged at Dallas's shirt, sliding it over his head. Bright, golden light shone through the window, lighting up his tan skin and making his double star tattoos stand out even more.

Dallas grabbed her waist, sliding his heated palms up the expanse of her skin under her shirt. His touch was rough, hurried.

Possessive.

Ava shimmied out of her leather coat, feeling the heat of the moment.

Dallas sucked at the flesh of her neck.

The motion caused Ava's eyes to close in ecstasy, but in the dark confines of her mind, she imagined someone else. Memories of Cassius's lips on her wrist, his tongue against her flesh, assaulted her, mixed with the sensation of Dallas's lips on her skin.

Her thighs clenched in response, wetness blossoming between them as the memory of fangs piercing her skin danced with the desire to feel such perfect bliss again. She moaned in response, feeling a mixture of guilt and need. She didn't want to think about Cassius.

Not now, not ever.

But it seemed the sinfully delicious vampire who remembered how she liked her coffee had a hold on her that would never cease.

Not until she could remove his mark.

Ava opened her eyes, noticing the faint sparkle on her skin from where he had bitten her. Dallas worked at the buttons of her jeans, and she did not stop him.

"That's what I thought, Kitten. You know who you belong to," Dallas growled in her ear.

"Jake..." she groaned, feeling her heart catch in her throat.

"Tell me you're mine."

She could feel the tears starting to pool in her eyes.

The guilt, the pain... he was

supposed to make it go away.

He always made it go away, so why was this time different?

Dallas slid her jeans off, throwing them across the room. The cold air of the kitchen kissed her skin, shocking her like ice.

He grabbed her neck, imploring her eyes with his.

"Who do you belong to?" he asked again, his voice heavy with command, with need. The words were no different than what she'd heard over the last two years. After all, Dallas delighted in dominating her and up until this very moment, she'd been more than happy to receive his rewards and punishments in the privacy of their stolen moments.

But something in the way his words sounded now, how his voice trembled in the slightest, it was as if he was asking her for more than just sexual consent.

When he fingers slid his beneath her panties, caressing her slick folds before diving in, she cried out in ecstasy. The slow drag as he slid them in and out of her was mind-boggling and she could feel her orgasm starting to culminate, making her feel foggy, unfocused. She longed for release, to be set free once more.

Her words came easily, but they felt empty.

"You, Jake. I belong to you."

"That's right, Kitten," he growled as he slid her panties down her legs over her ankles and boots. The cool stone of the countertop was soothing to the heat radiating throughout her.

"And I'm going to make sure you

don't forget it, do you understand?" His voice was dark and called to the demons inside of Ava she thought she'd buried. The sound of his belt and pants hitting the tile floor echoed around her like a church bell, loud and ominous.

Ava closed her eyes, nodding in response. "Yes. I understand."

At that moment, she did not understand what Dallas was truly saying. She only focused on the familiarity of the action itself. After all, it wasn't the first time they'd gone about this song and dance.

She'd given herself to Dallas plenty of times. He needed to know he was in control, that she was at his mercy. And for two years, she'd found solace in their arrangement because for the sliver of however long it lasted, with Dallas she could be free.

Free of the ghosts that haunted her, the burdens that had become so heavy for her to carry.

Memories surfaced. Hazy, blurry memories of burning buildings, blood, and deep, satisfying pleasure. In the space of her consciousness, all she could see was bright green eyes, and sharp, pointed fangs.

And when Jake Dallas entered her in a swift, sharp motion, Ava cried out as she held onto the memory of Cassius's bite like a life raft. Nothing would ever feel as blissful, and she hated that.

Dallas slid his hand underneath her thigh, hooking her legs around his hips as he thrust into her with steady force. Ava held onto to Dallas's large shoulders, her fingernails digging into his warm skin as he picked up his pace. She could feel his control slipping, and her own fading into darkness. She was so very close to the edge she felt as if she might fall. Into the darkness, into *him,* so far that she would lose herself.

Dallas took her face in his hands, bringing his lips to hers as he stilled, spilling himself inside of her.

When he pulled away, leaving Ava dripping wet and unsatisfied, alone on his kitchen counter without another word, Ava could feel herself shatter like the glass of whiskey on the floor into a million pieces.

# CHAPTER SIXTEEN

CASSIUS LOOKED OVER his shoulder, expecting to see Malcolm, but the older Crowley was nowhere in sight.

The bar was not packed, but it was busy for a mid-morning shift with various tables filled with women sharing appetizers and mimosas. It dawned on him that save for Malcolm, himself and the bartender, he hadn't seen any males in the establishment, only cementing the older Crowley's suspicious actions and claims of a nest.

He did not trust Malcolm entirely, not in the way he trusted Ava. For better or for worse, he and Ava were bound in a sense, and he had a feeling he'd trust her, mark or no mark. But her brother was another story.

Though Cassius had done all he could to prove to both Ava and her brother he was not a threat, the man did not take any liberties with his feelings on the matter.

He'd been far too amicable when they'd discovered one another, looking almost nonplussed that Ava and he had shown up on *their case.* He knew Malcolm was using him, but to what end he was not certain.

Amora tugged on Cassius's arm as

she led him through the bar, through the kitchen to a small office where once in, she closed the door. The room was small, only big enough to fit a small loveseat among a desk with scattered papers and used mugs of what smelled like stale coffee and blood.

"I thought you were dead, Cassius," she said softly as she locked the door.

In the small space, Cassius felt only slightly claustrophobic.

"In a way, I was. Dead, that is," he said as he traced his fingers along the messy desk nonchalantly, looking for what he was not sure. He only knew that whatever it was, it would stand out when he saw it. A name, a printout, perhaps a sticky note with a *Bryan is here!*

Amora slowly made her way over to him, forcing him to look at her.

Bountiful blonde curls spilled over her cleavage and she looked up at him with deep, forest green eyes. The way she was looking at him was familiar. Too familiar, and Cassius felt a tinge of panic.

Had he traded a fox's den for a lion's instead?

"So much has happened since..." Her voice was sweet, carrying the hint of ner native French accent.

Cassius pursed his lips, but he did not break her gaze. He felt as if he was on a cliff, and the wrong word, the wrong movement would surely throw him over the edge. Give Amora the wrong idea.

But a part of him still felt sentimental toward the Medici queen. After all, they'd once been friends, and he considered her an ally. And for a brief time... they were perhaps a bit more. But Cassius did not want to think about such things. He wanted to let sleeping dogs lie.

"How are your children?" he said, changing the subject.

Amora shrugged. "Donatello is fine. Stirring up a ruckus in Paris like his father at his age. Lilibet is in Spain with her father, Thomasse, wanting nothing to do with me, but isn't that the will of daughters anyway?" She rolled her eyes. "Henry met an untimely death. Hunters."

"You... took other consorts?" Cassius could hear the weight of that word, heavy in the air.

*Consort.*

He'd almost been one himself. Amora had unofficially propositioned him all those years ago, when he and Eden were... together. Yet, if Eden had succeeded in rising to such stature as a queen herself, if she hadn't told him the truth...

Is that where he would be now?

Would he be the consort to the Boracellis his father couldn't be?

By Eden's side living in the luxury of the high covens, father to a small brood of powerful little vampires?

The thought made Cassius pale, made his blood run ice cold. For remembering those moments with Eden was far too painful. The life he'd been sentenced to was full of desire, hunger, pain, and lies. So many lies he'd been naive to believe.

"I had to. Luckily, I'd given birth to Donatello when Marcellus was alive, so that bought me my spot on the Medici throne in his absence, but..." Amora looked away, and he could see the strain in her jaw. "Had I not had our son, I would have been easily replaced, and they would have had to institute a new, fresher model as those archaic rules state." Amora tossed her hair behind her shoulder, looking away for a moment as if she too were remembering a painful past.

Cassius's heart broke for a moment, thinking of all the things she must have had to endure while he hid in the shadows. He'd never gotten the chance to truly tell her how sorry he was about what had transpired with her consort, Marcellus.

The only man Eden ever truly loved.

He felt a sting of guilt that while he'd been on the run, finding a suitable place to disappear, Amora not only had to mourn her consort, but fight tooth and nail to keep the spot on the throne she deserved.

"A queen is only as good and powerful as the heirs she provides." Her voice cracked at the words, and Cassius wanted to reach out. Pull her into his arms and hug her.

He understood all too well what it was to be beholden to ancient laws and forced bloodlines. Though immortal, they were but slaves to their own blood as well as the life source humans provided. Only the strongest of bloodlines prevailed, the high covens practically untouchable. All the other bloodlines were diluted and would never be as strong as the pure Medicis, Aurelias, and of course, the Boracellis. Though there were others, even they paled in comparison of wealth and standing.

His Aurelian bloodline was highly coveted for its purity and the ability to sire—an ability that was much rarer these days—and produce viable, blood born heirs was both a blessing and a curse to Cassius. It was the reason he'd grown up a secret, the reason Eden had been betrothed to him, and it was one of the main reasons he left the life of the glittering high covens.

He wanted more than the life of a consort, bound to another in a loveless arrangement that the only use was to provide strong, powerful heirs. When Eden had come clean, it had been a blessing. The way out was more than clear, but it came with its costs.

"Unless you are the Boracelli queen." Amora's words were thick with bitterness, pulling him from his melancholy thoughts.

"She is... still..."

"Queen? Yes. Childless? Yes. No consorts either, just blood slaves."

The words made Cassius nauseous. He'd heard about Eden's rise to the throne when it happened, and his heart was conflicted. It was what she always wanted, but knowing she fought Francesca, eliminating her... it did not sit well with Cassius.

How many innocent lives had she taken?

How many people had she stabbed in the back, bought their alliance in order to slay a sitting queen?

Amora took a step closer, reaching her hand out to caress Cassius's cheek.

"Your mother is well. I can... get word

to her if you would like?" she whispered.

Cassius could not fight the undeniable stirring in his stomach.

"She is still in Eden's possession?" Cassius felt his voice shake, but he needed to know.

Amora nodded, tracing her fingers over his jaw, and he could not help but settle his hand over hers as she did so. He looked at her with pain, guilt, and concern as he waited her answer.

"She is. But I have allies, Cassius. My reach is far."

The chill of her skin against his palm was somewhat soothing and he knew better. This is who Amora was.

Calculating.

Manipulative.

Alluring.

It was a wonder she herself was not a

siren Djinn, for she was just as tempting.

Cassius shook his head. If his mother was safe, that was all he needed to know. Despite Amora's promise, he knew allies could be bought, and Eden was not a forgiving woman. If one breath of his name reached her ear...

"I can not risk that, but I appreciate the gesture," he said as he dropped his hand to his side, feeling the guilt over his decision all over again.

"Oh Cassius..." Amora's eyes sparkled with intensity.

"After all these years, you are still so stubborn aren't you?" She let out a laugh as she pulled away, heading to the chair behind the desk.

"Old habits die hard, *Ami.*"

Amora giggled. "Oh, that is just a

nickname my... employees gave me."

"Employees?" Cassius was confused.

Amora sat back in her chair, crossing her legs as she focused her gaze on him.

"Well, a single mother of two needs a hobby, darling. It was either this or a casino and I rather detest all those blinking lights and buzzing machines."

Cassius shook his head.

*Still the same old Amora.*

*Restless and full of ambition.*

"And what kind of *hobby* do you have in which you have employed sirens like Enchantress?"

"How do you know Caroline?" Amora's voice was no longer sweet and flirtatious. It was full of seriousness.

Cassius slid his hands in his pockets as he walked closer to her, leaning against her desk.

*Down to business, finally.*

"Enchantress?" he asked.

Amora nodded. "Yes, Enchantress is her handle, but I prefer to address my employees by their given names. It feels more... personal."

"I've seen her on AltGothGirls.com."

Amora laughed, the sound saccharine. She grabbed a coffee cup, taking a long pull before answering him. When her tongue licked crimson liquid from her lips, Cassius's throat constricted, his stomach turning with hunger.

"Oh dear Cassius, have you fallen that far?" she teased as she rose from her chair, closing the space between them.

"I have not fallen at all, Amora. That is the point." The words fell out of his mouth without warning. The lines of past and present were starting to blur.

"You always did have a type, I suppose." She offered him the cup.

Cassius stared at it, the smell of fresh blood like sweet honey.

His cock twitched in his leather pants and his stomach turned. He needed to eat, soon.

"And what type is that?" Cassius looked at the beautiful woman in front of him, offering him exactly what he needed at the moment, and he fought the compulsion to take her offer.

"Tall, dark, and bitter. Like black coffee. Incapable of giving you everything you deserve."

Her free hand slid around his waist, playing with the loops of his pants.

He'd always found Amora attractive,

found her warm and comforting even in some of his darkest days.

But she was as much a predator as Eden. They only wore different crowns.

Cassius steadied his gaze as he pushed the cup of blood away.

"I'm on a diet. I do not feed on the living, anymore."

Amora shrugged as she drained the last of the blood, and Cassius stifled a groan. She set it down on the ledge of the desk.

"Always so noble," she purred. "Here we are centuries later, free of our bindings, and still you deny your instincts. You haven't changed at all."

She settled her hand over the small of his back, and he did not move. He couldn't.

It was as if he was paralyzed, but he

knew no vampire other than Eden possessed such an ability.

"We are never free, petite étoile."

Amora slid her hand up his back as she pulled him closer. In her eyes, he could see yesterday, visible and bright.

*The glittering chandeliers.*

*The fountains of blood.*

*Amora's reflection in the mirrors as they danced across the floor like ghosts in a haunted ballroom.*

*His reflection in the mirrors of her bedchambers as they lay entangled together in her sheets.*

"Freedom is an illusion, Cassius. The rabbit thinks it is free of the fox, but as fast as it is, it will never outrun its predator."

Every bone in Cassius's body told him to run. Run far away from Amora and her pretty, pink claws. But he also knew in the depths of his soul that Amora was the fastest way to uncover what he'd come to Ohio to do. Find his friend. If her reach truly was as far as she advertised, then she'd know exactly where his friend would be, given Enchantress was her *employee*. Unless of course, Enchantress—Caroline—had gone off script, which could be a possibility.

"Is that so?" he purred, pushing away his instincts and his own qualms. He knew the way to Amora's heart was rather like picking up a motorcycle after nearly thirty-some years, and he also knew he could catch more flies with honey than with vinegar. This game of cat and mouse was familiar. Eden detested games, but Amora... Amora loved the *chase.*

Amora smiled wickedly at him as she nodded, leaning up on her tiptoes to meet Cassius's lips. It was a strange feeling, like time had somewhere gotten away from him while at the same time he'd fallen back to yesterday, to Paris in the 1800's. Her body pressed against his did nothing to quell the bloodlust that had formed in his being, his hunger recognizing a means to an end despite his best efforts. Amora tasted of sour blood and cherries.

*Like a cherry danish.*

Images pushed forth Cassius could not fight, nor did he want to. He knew the answer lay on the other side of Amora's sweet kiss, but he wished in that moment, that she was someone else. That the lips that parted for him, inviting his tongue into her mouth, belonged to a wicked slayer, a woman whose kiss he was certain would taste like heaven itself, and not of sour blood and mistakes.

Amora let out a soft moan against his lips, and he knew he had her.

"You are hungry," she whispered, biting her bottom lip.

Cassius sighed, regrettably acknowledging the truth.

"Starving, actually," he whispered.

Amora's eyes glowed with excitement.

"Perhaps I have just the thing to sate your hunger, *Mon étoile*," she cooed as she slid her hand into his.

# CHAPTER SEVENTEEN

AVA COULD NOT fathom how much time had passed. Her mind spiraled, trying to figure out where she'd gone wrong, where things had changed, and she could not pinpoint it. Though Dallas had left her feeling guilty on plenty occasions, he'd never left her feeling so empty, so unfulfilled before.

Ava buttoned her jeans, catching her disheveled reflection in the sleek silver of

Dallas's refrigerator door, and she had to turn to look away.

The woman staring back at her was not one she recognized.

She kicked the broken glass on the floor aside with the heel of her boot as she stuffed down the pain, the shame, and the guilt, locking it all in a coffin at the bottom of her soul with the rest of her demons.

Dallas sat on his couch, shirtless. He leaned his large, muscular arms over his knees, tapping away on his phone. Dressed in a pair of fresh jeans, she could see his hair was wet from a recent shower. The room was soft, boasting the same white and gray color scheme, accentuated by dark indigos, bright ochres and pale blue accents. It looked like something out of a magazine.

"You going to tell me what exactly you and my brother are up to, or am I wasting my fucking time?" she bit as she leaned against the wall, keeping her distance.

A part of her ached for him. To throw herself around him and apologize. To placate this man who held her to such a higher standard, who tried irrefutably to break her defiance.

But the larger part of her wanted to walk away from it all. From him, from the graves she needlessly dug to keep her secrets buried. She was plain and simply, tired.

Dallas ran his hand over his face, shaking his head before turning to look at her and setting the phone down on the coffee table.

In his bright blue eyes, all she could

see was pain.

But Ava would not run into the arms of a hurricane so soon after destruction.

She knew better.

"Your brother seems to think the Djinn and the vamps are working together." He sighed, wringing his hands together. In the light of the living room, sitting on the pale gray couch, he looked every bit his age. But he did not look like he belonged anywhere but on the back of a motorcycle, chasing sunsets and sunrises.

"It's never a simple thing, is it?" she asked.

Dallas spoke softly. "No, I guess not."

Ava fixed her gaze on the attractive, freshly-showered Dallas, the scent of his Old Spice bodywash thick in the air. "And you haven't taken them out yet?

You two must be loosing your magic."

Dallas shifted his stance, looking at her with sad eyes.

"You can sit down, you know." He spoke evenly.

"I'm good where I'm at, thanks," she sternly replied.

Dallas pursed his lips as he nodded.

"Ava, I'm…"

Just as he opened his mouth to speak, the front door opened to reveal a grinning Malcolm, who strolled in and plopped himself down on the couch across from Dallas, kicking his feet up on the coffee table.

"What the fuck has you so happy?" Ava bit as she turned to look for someone else.

"Where's Cassius?" she asked, feeling strangely panicked.

Malcolm looked happy as a clam as he clasped his hands in his lap. "Catching us some big fish." Malcolm smiled. "You know, Dad always taught me you catch bigger fish with bigger bait."

Ava felt her blood chill.

*If he laid one finger on him, I will kill him myself.*

*That monster is mine to slay.*

"So you went to the Clam?" Dallas spoke.

Ava watched as his demeanor shifted, like nothing had happened.

Nothing had happened. Nothing out of the ordinary anyway. It wouldn't be the first time they'd gotten into a heated argument that ended up in sex.

So why did his dismissal, his change of character make her feel so small, so insignificant?

They'd been quiet about their affair for the last two years, but in all honesty, they'd been keeping secrets since he and Malcolm had discovered she'd been bitten. Everything was the same as it always was, except... it wasn't. Something had changed. Between them, in herself.

"I got a good look at the place, and it's crawling with Djinn."

"No vamps?" Ava asked, shifting her focus to her brother.

Mal nodded. "Well, there was one vamp." He snickered.

"Real pretty thing, too." He whistled before continuing. "My money says she's the ring leader. I have to say, your little vampire puppy seems to have some game. She ate him like he was fucking filet mignon."

Ava's lips strained into a straight line.

Why did her brother's words make her feel so cold?

"And you just left him there?" Dallas asked, his voice rising.

Malcolm smiled. "Of course. Your bike's equipped with a tracker."

Dallas's eyebrows furrowed and Ava looked between them, sensing the next hurricane was coming.

"You let the fucking bloodsucker touch my baby?" he grit out through his teeth.

"Honestly, I was surprised he knew how to drive the thing. Thought I was going to have to get all up close and personal."

"Wait... so... Cassius knows how to drive a motorcycle?" Ava asked, dumbfounded.

"That's your takeaway?" Dallas bit at her.

Ava shrugged. "What can I say? I have a thing for leather pants and bikes," she nipped back at him, if only to wound him. The desire, the instinct to rub salt in Dallas's wounds was prevalent and she was feeling quite on edge. She hadn't had enough coffee for all this bullshit.

Malcolm rolled his eyes, knowing she wasn't serious.

At least, as far as he knew she wasn't serious.

Though she had to admit, she did like riding on the back of Dallas's motorcycle and she could not deny Cassius looked good in leather pants, despite being an annoying bloodsucking pain in her ass.

A startling thought pushed through her shock. "Wait... if we didn't show up... if you didn't have Cas... who would have been the bait?" she asked, looking between them.

Dallas's jaw tightened and she could tell he was grinding his teeth.

"D, of course." Mal shrugged. "He's always the bait when it comes to the pretty monsters."

Something about her brother's words made Ava hot all over. She never pretended to be unaware of the normal day to day operations the Goon Squad partook in, and she and Dallas had never discussed jobs outside of the ones they worked together.

But the reality of what went on while he was away... from her... both pissed her off and made her feel even worse.

Knowing Dallas was out there sidling up to vampires, trapping them with his roguish good looks, his dark, commanding voice, and his sex appeal.

It wasn't any different than what she did, so why did the realization of such things make her want to drive a stake through every vampire he'd cornered, when she knew damn well he'd ended their life himself?

Ava felt flush, and she knew she needed to get out of the claustrophobic cottage. She needed air, for she felt like she couldn't breathe.

"Where are you going?" Dallas asked as she turned heel and headed for the door.

"Out," was all she said as she ran down the front steps of the porch, racing to the car. She turned on the ignition, peeling out of Dallas's driveway with lightning speed, in search of sanity once more.

She pulled her phone from the dashboard where it lay, glowing with notifications.

*Meet me at The Sweet Shoppe. We need to talk.*

Ava stared at the text from *Cas*. She found herself wondering what he'd gotten up to left to his own devices, with the *pretty blonde* Malcolm had described.

She also knew, it could be a trap. If he'd fed recently...

But as she thought such things, a part of her heart ached.

Surely, he wouldn't do such a thing... would he?

Guilt befell her at the thought of a

casualty that one of them could have prevented had they kept him closer. Malcolm had given him too much of a leash.

She decided it was best to see for herself, and besides, they were supposed to be working together, right?

At least, that was how she rationalized things.

Curiosity bested her and she did not desire to turn around and head back to *base* any time soon.

She needed to be as far away from Jake Dallas and his wildfire heart as possible.

# CHAPTER EIGHTEEN

CASSIUS LEANED AGAINST Dallas's motorcycle, the wind blowing his soft, golden hair into his eyes. He felt guilty for what he'd done, leading Amora on as he had, taking advantage of their history.

Was she right?

Was he just too stubborn?

Perhaps.

Amora had lost Marcellus, just as

Eden had, and though she'd paid her dues to the high covens, taken other consorts... fate had severed those bonds as well.

Like himself, she was alone.

Her words rattled around in his brain. He'd made so many mistakes in his long, immortal life. Trusting Eden, covering for Marcellus. Covering for Eden when he'd discovered the truth about her affair with Marcellus.

He'd used Amora to get back at her, knowing full well the Medici queen favored him.

And he'd used her again, only this time a man's life was at stake.

The memory of earlier that morning, as Amora clung to his back on his borrowed transportation, he knew what he was doing. He'd rationalized it was for the good of everyone, driving off to the Marquis with Amora for an early lunch. As it would appear, her *business* was the Marquis, but of course he should have known that. The ornate signage boasted a sort of Moulin Rouge aesthetic, a callback to their younger days in Paris.

*Amora tugged his hand through the Marquis, the masquerade bar.*

*"When we open, I plan to have the doorway like one of those sensory deprivation tunnels. Imagine walking through the darkness, into a room full of illusion, only to find such grandeur on the other side," she said wistfully as they entered a room full of mirrors.*

*"The door is—"*

*"A mirror. Yes. Of course, those invited to the opening will know how to reach the ballroom, but I suspect it could be rather*

*fun for the mortals in question. Apparently escape rooms are all the rage these days." She giggled, opening the door.*

*She was right. It was positively wondrous, with its vaulted ceilings and cavernous appearance. Incandescent amber lighting illuminated the room by baroque-esque sconces adorned on the mahogany walls. In the low light of the place, it looked like something from another time. The sleek mahogany bar and its black marble finishings, the crystal chandeliers dripping with golden finishings. The tufted red leather booths and chairs. When they came to the center, Cassius laid his eyes on the large terrarium.*

*"What is this?" he asked as he took in the sight of the oversized tank. He could*

*see through it; it looked like a living terrarium, with hedges set up like a labyrinth.*

*"That is my main attraction. The labyrinth."*

*"What is it for?" Cassius asked, his throat dry.*

*"My patrons can buy a spot in the labyrinth. Their spots—mortals, of course—will be placed in the labyrinth, and my employees as well as very generous benefactors with... generous donations... will have the chance to exert their long-lost instincts. To hunt."*

*Cassius's blood chilled.*

*"And how much does a spot cost?" he asked.*

*"For you, I would make an exception. That is, if you had a mortal to place."*

*She cooed as she pulled him through*

*the room, toward another door, unlocking it.*

*"Where are you taking me?" he asked, starting to feel as if he'd walked into a trap. She'd promised him blood, after all.*

*"My stock room. I don't keep my reserves in the Clam. Too risky."*

*"Reserves?" he asked.*

*"This isn't my first rodeo, Cassius. It is only my current one," she said as he followed her down the dark hallway. The basement smelled of death.*

*Bloody, rotting death.*

*His eyes befell the doors set in the walls, similar to cells or stables. They all held small slivers of windows.*

*"What are the pens for?" he murmured, strolling up to one. Though he had a feeling he knew the answer.*

*"For the spots, of course. Livestock*

needs to be kept and primed before the big event, after all."

"Primed how?" His voice dropped as he set his hand on one of the doors, peeking in through the window.

What he saw chilled his blood, made his slow, dying heart still.

Bryan was huddled in the corner. Though the room didn't look entirely in disarray, it looked just as ominous, boasting a bed and a small latrine. It reminded him of the prisons in the Bastille, only with better furnishings.

And just as Amora spoke, his eyes opened, and he stared at Cassius in shock. Cassius quietly, as indiscriminately as possible, held his finger to his lips. How he wished he could implore the man with his loyalty, tell him he would indeed find a way to bust him *out. Though he could not risk doing so with Amora watching, that he knew. He would simply have to convene with the Crowleys and Dallas, and they would have to make a plan.*

*Perhaps he could even use one of them as a spot...*

*"The Djinn of course. Give them a taste of heaven and then set them loose in the labyrinth. All men need something to chase too, you know."*

The sound of a purring Impala startled him from his thoughts. The blood bag Amora had given him was cold, much like that of the one he'd stolen from the Willowcrest Morgue. While Amora preferred live kills, she'd always been one to keep reserves, in times of scarcity. It appeared she hadn't changed, either.

He straightened his stance, the stolen pulse in his veins awakening with life once more. He felt a mixture of guilt and satisfaction. His thirst would be abated, for now.

Ava opened the car door, looking as breathtaking as ever in her band tee, her dark wash jeans, and jacket, and he felt as if he could finally breathe.

No matter what ghosts chased him, they all disappeared when he looked at her.

The woman he loved, who he'd lain claim to.

The woman who wanted to kill him six out of seven days of the week.

*You have a type.* Amora had said. Perhaps she was right on that account as well. After all, she wouldn't be the first woman he'd fallen for with a penchant for blood.

Ava sauntered over to him, scowling. She stood in front of him, but kept her distance. He did not miss that she did not look at him immediately, but instead her gaze fixated on the motorcycle he was leaning against.

*Dallas's motorcycle.*

"My brother said so, but I gotta say I had a hard time picturing it." She spoke plainly.

Cassius smiled. "And how did you picture it?"

"I mean, you're not exactly, like, the biker type. You're missing the muscles, not to mention the vest with some stupid ass graphic stitched on the back." She crossed her arms.

"I have many talents, my sweet Avarice, I can assure you."

"Mhmm. Better to lure your victims with. If they're into that sort of thing, I guess."

Cassius noted the annoyance in her voice.

"Are you hungry?" he asked. He knew if she did not have nearly a thousand calories of sugar or coffee before noon, she could get quite an attitude, though she would deny such things if he said them out loud.

Before she could even speak, her stomach answered him with a rumble.

"I'm fine," she bit. "You wanted to talk."

"Will coffee suffice, then?" He slid his arm out, his hand bracing against the painted seat.

Ava shifted her stance, bouncing her leg.

"Why don't you just tell me what you want, Cas?" she bit.

Cassius furrowed his eyebrows. Ava was always sarcastic and there was always a sort of venom in her voice when she talked to him, but something about her tone, about her body language, the way she was looking at Dallas's motorcycle...

Panic flooded him, mingling with a sort of possessiveness Cassius had never felt before. It made him hot, worried, and it stirred his bloodlust in an entirely new way.

The desire to reach out across the canyon between them and pull her into his arms was overwhelming. All he wanted was to comfort her, but he couldn't.

She would surely push him away,

threaten to stake him, or worse... maybe she would follow through on her threat in the obvious state of upset she was in.

Ava was temperamental on most days, let alone bad ones.

He wanted to persist, wanted to push further and ask her what had happened.

If Dallas hurt her somehow... The thought caused his bloodlust to fill him with a deep, burning desire to *kill*. The thought of sinking his fangs into Dallas's neck, snapping it until he heard the definitive crack, caused his cock to harden and his mouth to go dry. Mixed with his recent meal, the need to protect what was *his* was a primal desire he'd never felt before.

But Ava was not his.

Not really.

Her blood belonged to him, but he

knew it was only a matter of time before the hourglass would run out. She could never be his as he wanted her to be. His time with her was limited, and so he pushed the dangerous thoughts away, conceding to her demands once more.

He would always give her exactly what she wanted, whatever that may be, until the last grain of sand dropped from the hourglass.

"Bryan is alive," he said solidly. He pushed away from the motorcycle, taking one stop closer to her. "We do not have to stand out here in the cold. Come, let us go inside," he tried again, his voice gentle, as if he was talking to a frightened animal.

Ava glanced up at him, her amber eyes full of questions. Her stomach rumbled again.

"Fine. Pain in my ass." She rolled her eyes as she turned away from him, heading for the door.

Cassius smiled, but she could not see it.

"But you're buying this round!" she shouted as she opened the door.

Cassius slid his hands in his pockets.

"As you wish, my sweet Avarice."

***

Ava picked at her cherry danish, and Cassius felt a sting of guilt. The memory of Amora's lips on his, the thoughts that filled his brain, made him feel like a monster.

Ava tore a piece of flaky dough off, sighing in defeat.

"Where is he?" she asked quietly.

"He is in the Marquis. You were

right," Cassius answered her softly.

"And you just left him there? Some friend you are."

"He is under lock and key. I was not able to seize him myself at the moment. I was... indisposed."

Ava smirked, raising an eyebrow.

"With Vampire Barbie?" she bit, her tongue laced with familiar venom.

"I do not know what Malcolm told you but..."

"I don't care. All I care about is getting Bryan out safely." She took a long drink of her coffee.

Cassius watched her, feeling his stomach turn with hunger. The blood bag he'd swiped from the blood bank on the way to the Sweet Shoppe it seemed was not enough.

"Her name is Amora. She is... an

old... friend." He was careful with his words.

"I don't suppose this *friend* of yours would be amenable to just like, letting Bryan go?" she asked, twisting her lips.

Cassius shook his head. "I am afraid not. She has plans to use him as..."

What could he say?

Bait?

Vamp chow?

Entertainment?

"She owns the Marquis. There is a labyrinth inside which mortals will be... donated... as entertainment. Creatures like myself, will be able to pay a hefty price to chase them, to hunt... and the event will be visible to all the patrons of the masquerade as a show of sorts."

He watched as she sank her teeth into the red, cherry filled pit of her danish, some of it smearing along her fair skin.

Images of blood running down her chin pushed through his psyche, causing his cock to twitch. He crossed his legs, tightening them as he cleared his throat.

How was it something so simple caused him such detriment?

It was just a pastry for god's sake.

Though Cassius felt somewhat perverse that he often took enjoyment in watching Ava eat such things, if only because he knew inevitably she would end up with red jelly all over her perfect, luscious lips.

*Her lips look beautiful stained so red.*

Ava looked up at him as she swallowed the confectionary delicacy. Her gaze was full of fire.

"So what you're telling me is he's alive until he hits that labyrinth. How the hell do we get him out? Crash the place or..."

"That is the part I will need your help with. Well, I will need Malcolm and Dallas's help, too."

Cassius watched as Ava stiffened completely.

"We don't need them," she said too quickly.

Cassius did not miss her words. They hit him like a silver bullet.

"I thought you said there was no *we*, Ava," he said, his voice softened.

"Well, I can do this myself. I just thought *maybe* you'd want to..."

"Amora said she would make an exception for me. I could easily be a part of the games. It would be an inside job. Malcolm or Dallas could be the red herring, and we could work together, to rescue Bryan and escape the labyrinth. Though someone will need to be responsible for causing a distraction upstairs, I—" He stilled, realizing he was rambling too much, and he needed to tread lightly. Especially given the fact he'd already starting planning and arranging the rescue mission.

Ava huffed in annoyance.

"What is it Ava?" He cocked his head to the side, watching her expression fall.

"You know what, it doesn't matter. I don't need them, and I certainly don't need you," she said as she rose, grabbing her coffee.

"Ava..." His heart fell, seeing her in such turmoil. Something was wrong. He knew it in his bones. It wasn't as if they worked a lot of cases together, but enough that he knew she should have leapt at the chance to tell him all the faults with his plan and fabricate one herself. The way her mind worked always seemed to fascinate him.

"The Masquerade is a monster's ball. The patrons will be vampires likely of high stature. The Djinn will also be there, preying on the mortals. Enchantress isn't the only Djinn cultivating a population for this event," he said, just as she turned her back on him.

She stopped in her tracks, turning to face him once more. Ava looked back and forth, but she did not return to her seat.

Cassius rose, grabbing their napkins and garbage. He threw away the trash before moving over to her side. Of course, he left space between them, as he always had.

But every fiber of his being wanted to close that space, sidle up next to her and wrap his arm around her waist. To hold her, soothe her. Quell her fears and worries.

His throat felt dry as he looked at her, and he sucked in a deep breath.

Knowing what he was going to say next, he was not sure how she would react. She may be tempted to stake him as it was, and so he kept them both in public, in eyesight of the Sweet Shoppe cashier.

Ava's face paled.

"And *creatures* such as yourself get to hunt down victims like Bryan? Like a safari? How do I know I can trust you won't fuck us all over and devour the spots yourself?"

He did not miss the bite in her tone as she settled on the word trust.

"Because, Ava, I am not your enemy. Bryan is my friend, and I do not have many of those. I am a man of my word, and I promise you I will do everything in my power to protect all of you." He paused, gazing at her upon that one word, *you.* It carried so much weight, as he wished he could make her understand. He would never hurt her, or anyone she cared about. It was not within his nature, bond or no bond. She would always be safe with him. But his next words would likely sound suspicious, and so he sighed, knowing what he was about to say would potentially land him a stake in his chest, or worse, a punch to the gut.

"I bought a spot. To ensure us a way into the event."

"You what?" Her voice escalated, enough to garner the attention from a nearby janitor.

"We will have an easier chance this way."

Cassius motioned for her to follow him outside and she did, waiting for him to continue.

"Who are you planning on putting in the big monster royale, Cas?" she asked, pinching the bridge of her nose, squinting her eyes.

"I would prefer your brother. I have full confidence he would be able to hold his own against a room full of monsters and likewise victims."

Ava scoffed as she turned around, angrily opening the door.

Cassius followed her into the light of day like a moth to a flame.

"I bet I could take them," she bit.

Cassius smirked behind her. Of course she would feel emboldened by his denouncement.

She hurried down the steps toward her car, toward his current ride. He threw his leg over the seat, not missing her gaze as it flashed to his legs as he did so. The metal between his legs was a most welcome distraction from his strained cock.

Ava scoffed, crossing her arms as he started the motorcycle.

"Then who would distract them?" he purred.

Ava pursed her lips. "Is that all I'm good for? Vamp bait? Distractions? Just another pretty thing to turn heads?" Her tone was highly agitated.

"There are darknesses in life and there are lights, my sweet Avarice, and you... you are one of the lights. The light of all lights," he said, his heart in his throat. "Besides, I thought you would relish in getting a chance to dress up. It is a masquerade, after all."

"Did you seriously just fucking quote Dracula to me?"

Cassius smiled slyly. "Smart as a whip, too."

Ava rolled her eyes. "Whatever. Where the hell am I supposed to get a costume this last minute, *Dracula*?"

Cassius smirked. "You are resourceful. You'll figure something out."

"Mhmm."

Cassius kicked the stand up.

"Where are you off to now?" she

asked, her gaze roving over his arms, his fingers, as he gripped the handlebars. The stolen pulse in his veins *throbbed* with excitement.

Cassius's lips pulled back just enough to show a hint of fang, and her pulse raced within him. Ava could deny many things, but she could not deny her body's natural reaction to him. She could not deny the bond.

"Preparations must be made," he said smoothly.

Ava scoffed.

"I will keep you informed. In the meantime, speak with your brother and tell the lumbering oaf I will return his motorcycle in one piece. I know he must be beside himself without it."

"You trying to tell me what to do, Cas?" She smirked at him, her eyes lighting up with interest.

*There is the light I know.*

"I would not dare do such a thing," he purred.

Ava waved him off.

"Thanks for the poison," she said as she opened her car door, but she did not get in immediately.

Cas nodded to her before taking off toward the setting sun.

# CHAPTER NINETEEN

AVA SLAMMED DOWN her whiskey, pushing it toward the portly bartender.

"Hit me."

The Drowned Clam was thick with patrons. Cassius's information, as helpful as it was, both angered her and made her more than appreciative. Whether she wanted to admit it or not, a part of her trusted him, and she knew that was dangerous.

As it turned out, the Djinn-filled bar actually served decent drinks, but they were not on a social call. Vinny had been more than helpful in providing them with the blueprints to the Marquis, despite being on a case himself. Malcolm sipped his own whiskey, raising an eyebrow.

"You okay, Simba? You seem a little... on edge."

"I live on the edge, Mal."

Mal shook his head as the sounds of some pop artist droned on about wanting attention and not anyone's heart.

Her gaze flickered across the room to Dallas, who was currently talking to a woman. A Djinn. She was tall, with the same dark features as Enchantress. Despite her handy vampire radar

Cassius had cursed her with, she'd learned vampires were easy to identify if one knew what to look for. Their skin carried a pale glow, their features practically model-esque, and a chill breeze often accompanied them. But in the presence of the Djinn, she felt nothing, which concerned her. The leggy Djinn with its arms around Dallas's neck looked young, and Ava wondered how old she truly was.

Dallas leaned in, whispering something in her ear, and she knew exactly what he was doing, what he was planning to do.

Amora had taken Cassius to the Marquis.

Enchantress had taken Bryan.

The idea that Dallas would be taken, sequestered alone with the creature made her blood boil.

*He'd never lay with a monster.*

But a part of her thought she'd never do so either, and at this point in her life, she'd been with at least one. The thoughts of a possessed Sam Kingsley threatened to push forth and Ava drank some more.

She'd done the same thing on countless occasions.

*If you can get close to them, you can kill them.*

The fact Dallas hadn't protested to being a honeypot, or even blinked an eye at the suggestion, left Ava more than bothered. It was as if he truly did not care who his mark was, as long as the outcome ended favorably.

Ava needed to stake something, and at this point she did not care if it was a creature of the night or a thirty-five year old mortal who knew how to get underneath her skin.

"I swear it's like shooting fish in a barrel sometimes." Mal shook his head as he nodded at Dallas.

"You think creatures that old would have better taste," Ava bit.

"You two have been at each other's throats all evening. What happened? Dallas piss in your cornflakes?" he teased her.

"Nope," she said as the bartender gave her another drink.

Mal sighed as he looked around the room.

Ava's wrist suddenly flared with heat, goosebumps rising on her skin. She looked up to see Cassius, on the arm of a rather tall blonde who was dressed in a tight, pale pink bodycon.

She looked like a Playboy Bunny, or some erotic version of Elle Woods.

"He always gets shitty around her anniversary." Mal shrugged. "Don't take it personal if he's being a dick. It's normal for him this time of year."

"Anniversary?" Ava asked, never tearing her gaze off the leggy blonde sliding her hand in Cassius's. His smile was soft as he looked down at her, and she felt a twist in her stomach.

Her fingers ached to stake something.

To strike a match and watch a bitch burn.

It'd been too long since she'd felt the rush of death, since she'd watched a monster turn to ash.

She watched as Dallas slid his arm around his mark, pulling her aside with no remorse. He didn't even steal a glance at her, despite Ava's fiery gaze burning a hole into his back.

"Yeah. The anniversary of his wife's death. Always messes him up."

Ava's glass slid out of her hand and onto the floor, her heated blood going cold.

"What?"

"I thought you knew. You two have always been close, and I assumed when you were bitten he told you what happened."

"Nope. Guess we're not that close," she said, recovering quickly. The bartender grumbled as Ava slid some bills on the counter. She stepped over the glass, feeling only a little hazy. It wasn't enough, but she needed more than alcohol to settle her demons.

*Jake Dallas was married.*

Suddenly, the little blue cottage with the charming swing and magazine-worthy interiors made sense. Her heart caught in her throat as the memory rose from its ashes of their argument, of their heated moment, threatening to make her lose the whiskey she'd drank.

"You take the left. I'll take the right," Mal said as he slid his own bills on the counter.

Ava nodded, but his words didn't stick. She made her way through the crowd.

"Ava?" Cassius's voice stopped her dead in her tracks.

She turned, her vision jarring for a moment. The light above him cast an angelic glow on his the planes of his face, taking her back to the night he'd saved her.

The night he bit her.

He'd come from the shadows, all glowing eyes and sex appeal, and she thought he'd been an angel then.

How very wrong she was.

"Cas..."

"I did not expect to see you here... are you... alone?" he asked as he guided her toward a corner booth, away from Dallas and his target. She huffed in annoyance, wanting nothing more than to run away from Cassius, toward the shadows where she knew salvation lay in the form of her stake.

She knew this playbook by heart.

Lure the monster, get close.

Stake, burn.

Though according to Hunter and his extensive research, Djinn needed a silver blade and not a stake. Thankfully, she kept a set of etched silver knives in her trunk, not to mention her brother and Dallas kept a steady supply in the Chevelle as well.

It wasn't like Dallas needed her help, but if she didn't quiet the need to kill something soon, she was sure she'd explode.

"No. I'm not," She bit.

Cassius leaned closer, looking at her with concern.

"Perhaps we should convene elsewhere, discuss our... plans... for tomorrow. Together."

Ava huffed in annoyance as Dallas rounded the corner with Malcolm behind him, sans Djinn.

*Damn it!*

Something in the way he spoke, the

way he looked at her, made her blood rush, made the hair on the back of her neck stand. He looked at her the way she looked at whiskey.

As if just one hit could cure all of life's problems.

Ava turned to see Dallas's bright blue eyes staring at her from across the room. She watched the two hunters make their way through the crowd of humans, vampires, and Djinn.

"Barbie going to let you off your leash?" She could hear the fury, the frustration in her voice.

"You are not the only one with allies, Ava."

She did not miss the way his gaze flashed to her lips, or the way his tongue licked his lips, inciting deep desires Ava did not wish to acknowledge.

Not here, not now.

The crowd roared as some country song came over the airways, the singer droning on about saving a woman if she falls made Ava feel even more keyed up.

"I do not have, nor do I need, *allies*. All I need is my fucking stake and nothing else. Ever," she said.

Cassius crossed his arms, regarding her with concern once more.

"Blood will not satisfy you forever, Ava."

"Forgive me if I don't take the word of a fucking vampire when it comes to blood and death."

Dallas and Malcolm met them in the center of the floor.

"We need to talk," Cassius said, his glowing green emeralds fixated on her.

On *only* her.

Dallas grumbled, "Not here."

Cassius nodded in the opposite direction. "I have just the place."

***

The scent of grease and sugar was nauseating to Ava. Perhaps the whiskey she'd consumed was not helping either.

At this hour, the Waffle House was empty. Save for a drunk man in the corner snoring away and a couple of teenagers high off their asses giggling like children.

"The Marquis Masquerade's grand opening will start at nine. Bryan and the other spots will likely be loaded into the labyrinth around ten. Amora plans on getting everyone loosened up first, give their instincts a chance to come out."

Malcolm nodded. "So how does this

work? We just show up together or..."

"I will need to present you to Amora myself. Preferably, *before* the event so you may be... primed."

"Like fucking cattle," Dallas bit as he leaned back in the booth, glaring at him.

"The spots will be primed by the Djinn. From what I have gathered, that means that they will likely be looking into your head for what you desire most. They need a carrot to dangle so you will run, chasing a wish while we chase blood."

Ava crossed her legs underneath the table, her foot bouncing with anxiety.

"Fan-fucking-tastic," Mal bit.

Ava didn't like any of this, but she knew it was a means to save her friend. Still, it felt as if Cassius was leading them all into a trap.

He'd told her to trust him, but could she?

Could they?

Being in the same space with the hunters and the vampire who bit her was starting to make her feel more than queasy.

It was as if her worlds were colliding and she'd only just realized they were separated.

Her heart raced as she shifted away from Cassius. She was practically on the edge of the booth as was.

"Would you prefer to be the bait, Dallas? You looked quite comfortable earlier, or is that just with women you want to sleep with?"

Ava felt her blood turn to ice. She never wanted to vacate a Waffle House so bad in all her life.

She fought to control her facial expression. Cassius had no clue about her and Dallas, nor did her brother.

He was only making an observation. He must've seen Dallas and the Djinn earlier at the Clam, and put two and two together.

If looks could kill, Dallas would have murdered Cassius on the spot.

"I don't fuck monsters. I have morals."

"So you say, but I have seen no evidence of such things," Cassius said smoothly.

"I need you to get Bryan out and that's all that matters," Ava said, cutting through the thick tension that had somehow formed.

"Of course, Ava," Mal softly reassured her. "We'll get him out. And take out some fucking ticks and Djinn while we're at it," he said, his tone cocky as hell. Where her brother got his confidence, she was not sure, but at the moment she wished she had some.

"And what about Mal? How can I trust you'll get *him* out?" Dallas bit, grinding his teeth. Ava could see the tension in his jaw, how his fist shook.

Cassius sat straight, folding his hands on the table. He glanced at Ava before speaking.

"Because I am a man of my word. I do not make promises I can not keep. I know you do not trust me. I know you very well may try to kill me yourself, though you will find I am not as easy a target as the women you lure, but I digress. I will do everything in my power to protect you." Cassius looked at Ava for a moment before fixing his sight on Malcolm and Dallas.

"Because I am not your enemy. I am your ally, and I always have been."

Ava could stand no more as she got up, heading for the door.

"Ava..." Cas's voice was smooth like silk and she hated how it nearly stopped her in her tracks.

After this job, she vowed to put as much space as possible between her and the vampire who was starting to affect her more than she wanted to admit.

Her heart was in her throat as his words ricocheted through her.

How was it his words carved such a deep cut?

Memories of blood and fire surfaced, begging to pull her under.

*Burning pain in her neck radiated*

*throughout her blood, and she felt powerless as the Incubus toxin overtook her.*

Dallas had been right there, fighting the monster who'd hurt her. Trying to protect her. But he'd failed.

And in that moment, it dawned on her. She hadn't called for him.

She'd called for someone else.

Her memory was hazy, and she was told it was because of the fever from the toxin, mingling with antidote. She'd never remembered it clearly, but suddenly it all made sense.

Panic surged through her, and all she wanted to do was run. Run back to the Clam, find a vampire or Djinn to slay and quiet the uncertainty, the fear in her heart.

*Cassius pushed a stray strand of hair*

*behind her ear, his touch cold, yet gentle.*

"Ava!" Dallas hollered as she burst through the door into the empty parking lot, feeling as if her lungs were going to explode. She welcomed the cool air, closing her eyes.

"Leave me the fuck alone, Jake!" she hollered back.

"Ava, look at me," he commanded.

Tears formed at the edges of her eyes and she could not stop them.

"No! You don't get to do this!" she said as she turned around, looking at him with anger.

So much anger.

Dallas strode toward her, closing the space between them. He grabbed her by the neck, pulling her closer.

"Dallas, stop... they'll see," she whispered.

"I don't fucking care, Ava. I don't. I'm done hiding. I... I love you, Ava I'm sorry."

She shook him off.

"Love me? You're not supposed to love me!" she yelled. Her blood raced, and the tears fell freely. "That was the deal, remember? No feelings."

"I didn't fucking want this either!" he growled.

Ava ran her hands over her face in frustration. She hated crying. Crying meant she was weak.

And Ava was not weak. She killed monsters for goodness sake. But yet, in the overbearing presence of this man she was broken.

"You say you have my back. That you want to protect me. But throwing yourself into a locked box with a bunch of fucking monsters is not protecting me."

"And you'd throw your brother in there?" Dallas bit. "Put your own flesh and blood at risk? Why don't you volunteer, huh? Or would your pussywhipped little vampire have a fucking problem with that?" he snapped.

"Leave Cas out of this. He has nothing to do with it."

"Are you really that fucking stupid? He has everything to do with it, Ava. You should have killed him a long time ago."

Ava felt a part of her snap, the last stitch coming undone as she got in Dallas's face, pointing her finger at him.

"It's no different than when you fucking dangle yourself in front of monsters, Dallas. Besides, I can trust my brother. I can't say the same about you anymore, can I?"

His eyes darkened at her words.

"Since when do you not trust me?" He gritted his teeth.

The cold wind was like ice on her skin.

"Were you ever going to tell me you were fucking married?" She felt herself falling apart at the seams.

Would he stitch her back together or cut the threads?

The moment she said the words, she wished she hadn't.

Dallas looked as if he could barely breathe.

He looked... hurt.

"Ava... I..."

The memories broke into a million pieces as they spiraled to the ground.

*Dallas yanking her by her long*

*ponytail into his arms, his brutal kiss like a match to gasoline.*

*His anger when he'd found out she'd slept with Sam, the Incubus.*

*His jealousy when he'd cornered her in Howlers the night they'd crossed the line. After Sawyer hit on her.*

*The grip of his fingers entangled in her hair, his dick down her throat.*

*The pain in his eyes when he saw her scars, the deep cuts where she'd been attacked by vicious vampires, scars that healed because of Cassius's venom.*

*How Dallas turned her away in that moment, because she was damaged.*

*Broken.*

The tears streamed down her face, one fractured memory at a time.

*The sweat from their sparring matches covering her like armor.*

*The way he felt buried inside her, ravaging her with his lips, the rough sensation of his facial hair brushing her thighs.*

*The look in his eyes as she stared up at him, telling him she was his.*

*The way he made her forget everything, everyone. The way he smelled, like tobacco and whiskey and un kept promises.*

And for the first time Ava understood.

She'd fallen for Dallas, too, and she was more frightened of that than anything else. She could not afford to fall for anyone. Love was not in the cards for Ava Crowley. Love only meant death.

So she did the only thing she knew how to do.

She fought back.

"What? You wanted to what? To fuck

me until you forgot about her? About your pretty little white picket fence house and your former life?"

"Don't fucking talk to me like that," he roared. "Don't fucking talk about *my wife* like that!" He was enraged.

"What are you going to do about it? Fuck me into being your little good girl? Hmm? You going to dominate me until I fucking give in to your stupid Big Daddy Dallas bullshit? I got news for you Jake, I don't belong to you. I never have. So save me the drama. You want to fuck around and find out with the monsters, as far as I'm concerned that's where you belong because that's what you fucking are. A monster."

"Ava Marie Crowley, don't you fucking walk away from me."

Ava did not think twice as she turned

heel, walking toward the woods in search of the only thing that would truly quiet her pain.

Blood and ash.

# CHAPTER TWENTY

AVA'S HANDS SHOOK as she removed the stake from the nameless vampire she'd lured at the Drowned Clam. Blood ran down her stake, the scent pungent in the air. She shook, as the tears begged to come forth again.

Why did it still hurt?

She dropped her stake as she took out the matches from her jacket pocket. The smell of sulfur was welcome amidst the scent of decay, and she watched the flame settle, wavering in the darkness of night.

Ava paused for only a moment before she threw the match on the dark-haired vampire who'd been far too easy to catch. All it took was a little eye batting, a show of Cassius's bite mark, and they flocked to her like flies to honey.

It should have bothered her, how easy it was for her to kill.

But it didn't.

She'd been fighting forever. Fighting for peace within her mind, her heart. Her soul. No, Ava Crowley knew there were only two options, kill or be killed.

And she did not relish the idea of submitting to death so easily.

She watched as the flames engulfed bones, watched as the skin decayed before her very eyes in the middle of the forest.

He'd thralled her, the vamp with no name, and for a moment she wanted nothing more than succumb to it. The heat in her body, the lust in her belly. The desire to be had, to be worshipped for her blood, and to be free of the pain that would not relent.

But it wasn't the nameless vampire she wanted to be thralled by.

His thrall didn't feel... blissful.

His thrall didn't quiet the noise, and she suspected no vampire's thrall would ever feel as perfect as Cassius's.

She'd only felt it once, that very night, but it was enough to poison her thoughts forevermore.

When the last of the vampire's ashes blew away in the wind, she headed back through the woods to the Drowned Clam. Her hunger was not abated, though she wished it was.

*Perhaps a drink will help.*

Her phone vibrated in her pocket. She removed it, glancing at the screen.

She had four missed calls, one of them her brother.

The other three belonged to Dallas.

She swiped up on Malcolm's number, stopping just outside the door. Her brother picked up instantly.

"What the fuck? Where are you? Dallas said you blew up and left."

She pursed her lips.

"I'm fine Mal. I just needed a drink."

"You're not with that fucking tick, are you?"

Ava bristled at his words and their insinuation.

"No. When I left, Cassius was with you…"

"I don't know what you're running from, Ava, but whatever it is, you won't find the answer at the bottom of a glass. I know that better than anyone," his voice softened.

"That's the pot calling the fucking kettle black. You're the last one who should be giving me a lecture on running, considering you never come home."

Mal sighed.

"The boys called. After you ran off and Cassius left…"

Ava's blood chilled.

"They may have found something. Something we haven't tried…"

Ava braced herself the wall, her heartbeat stilling.

After all these years of searching for a way to break the mark... could it be they finally found something that would work?

"What is it?" she asked, feeling anxious but needing to hear the answer all the same.

"You are never going to believe this, but... blood of a Djinn."

Ava glanced at the door of the Drowned Clam, feeling as if freedom was finally tangible and the answer was on the other side of the door, in a room full of vampires.

But how did one catch a Djinn?

Would it be as easy as luring a vampire?

"That's it? What do I have to do, drink it?"

"Cut open the bite mark and spread

it. The Djinn are known for granting wishes, and that power comes from their blood."

"So if I open myself to their blood and wish really hard, it'll sever the bond?"

"Tito says it's a little more of a process than that, but yeah. That's the gist of it. Djinn's blood is highly powerful. Even among other supernatural beings." He paused.

"Come back to base, Ava."

"Thanks for calling, Mal. I'll talk to you in the morning."

"Ava don't hang up on me... Ava!"

Ava clicked the phone as a soft voice pulled her from her thoughts, heading into the Drowned Clam once more.

***

The world was starting to look rather

hazy after her third drink. She could still feel the blood on her hands, smell the scent of burning ash even though her hands were clean.

The Drowned Clam was much more vibrant at this hour, and she'd had no shortage of men willing to keep her cup full, and she was starting to feel numb. But numb was what she wanted.

She wanted to forget.

To be lost.

But she wasn't certain who was a mortal and who was a Djinn.

Smooth arms wrapped around her, pulling her close. She rolled her head back against the shoulder of a man whose name she could not remember. He felt... different. She knew it was dangerous. But danger was all she knew. There was no rest for the wicked, after all. She couldn't quite place it, but she would have bet he was a Djinn.

"Come with me," he purred in her ear.

Ava smiled wickedly as the alcohol hit its peak. He smelled good, felt good. She could feel her walls crumbling as his hand slid into hers, as his fingers brushed over her scar. She despised small talk, anyway.

"I thought you'd never ask," she said as she closed her eyes.

***

When Ava opened her eyes, she was in a dark room. Panic flooded her instantly as memories resurfaced of a nameless man, a sense of danger.

Of sharp teeth and rough hands, and regret.

Ava sat up in a bed, and she could

see she was not alone. She was half-dressed, missing her pants. The scratchy sheets fell to her waist and panic set through her. Bodies littered throughout the room were in various states of slumber, and her wrist heated with fire where fangs had laid claim on her blood four years ago.

One look around told her she was in a basement, and wherever she was, it was not well kept. She moved slowly, planting her feet on the floor. She was still wearing her panties, and for that she was thankful.

The air smelled of blood and sulfur. She turned to take it all in, her gaze falling on the body beside where she had been laying. Blood stained the sheets, and the memories assaulted her.

*The loud hiss, the bright blue glow of*

*the eyes of Djinn.*

Ava looked at herself in the broken mirror across from where she stood. She was covered in blood.

Dark, black, crimson blood.

Vampire blood.

Djinn blood.

She couldn't tell the difference.

She shakily held up her wrist. It did not look any different, save for the dried black blood stains on her skin.

Had she found the cure?

A sound pulled her from her thoughts, her concerns. A loud bang.

Ava quietly tiptoed over the bodies on the floor, most of them breathing. Her skin prickled like ice, her blood hot like liquid magma.

She opened the door to see a long, dark hallway, and the stone walls looked faded and old in the light. Voices sounded in the corridor and Ava hid against the wall.

It wasn't the first nest she'd been in, but it was the first time she'd woken up in a room full of monsters. The realization made Ava's stomach turn. She covered her hand with her mouth to keep from throwing up.

"The rest of the spots should be arriving soon," a man's voice said.

"We'll have to make sure the Djinn butter them up real good for the chase."

Ava stood still as a stone as realization overcame her.

Hadn't Cas mentioned the spots were to be delivered to the Marquis?

Was she...

The two creatures passed her and she held her breath. When she was certain they had disappeared, Ava set out down the corridor, looking for a way out. Door after door, it seemed the exit was nowhere to be found, and Ava wondered if perhaps she had been too careless. If she could not get out... Ava stamped her foot, cursing under her breath as she pinched the bridge of her nose.

*Think, Ava.*

*Think!*

She looked up toward the ceiling, praying for a sign, an answer. Instead, she only saw a clear ceiling, or rather... a floor. Above her, all she could see was glass, a giant terrarium. Plants and walls lined the space and Ava'a breath caught in her throat.

*The labyrinth.*

*That's where Mal and Cas will be...*

A creak sounded and she stopped

dead in her tracks. Her head was pounding, her heart racing.

"Wake up the others. We're going to need the room."

Ava could see the sliver of light from above, and she knew it was her ticket out. She nearly tripped over a broken piece of brick, the sound echoing in the space.

"You hear that, Romulus?" the voice called, sniffing the air.

"I smell a human."

Ava held her breath, picking up the brick and throwing it down the opposite end of the hall.

When the vampires took off in the other direction, Ava sprinted toward the light, hoping to reach her brother in time.

# CHAPTER TWENTY-ONE

CASSIUS PADDED DOWN the steps of Amora's condominium toward the kitchen. Sunlight filtered through the windows. He ran his hand through his golden hair, feeling tired. He did not need sleep, but sometimes he wished he could truly rest.

He texted Malcolm. Today was the day. Everything needed to be in place and he would have to present Malcolm to Amora this afternoon, so that there would be enough time to get Malcolm in the building. Thanks to one of the other hunters, Mal had disclosed he had blueprints to the place, which would help in their escape.

All that was left after that was making sure Ava and Dallas were on the same page.

The plan was rather simple.

When the Marquis opened, Ava and Cas would cause a distraction and slip downstairs. Amora had agreed to let him in to the labyrinth, excited at the prospect of watching Cassius channel his instincts, and he knew a way in was not an issue. Rather, it would be making it through the labyrinth untouched and with his collective that would be challenging, but Cassius was not all that unfamiliar with the odds stacked against him. Fate as it seemed, always underestimated him.

Dallas would be on the bottom level, ready to receive them and guard their transports and Ava would be safe, with him, away from the labyrinth. Though he hadn't disclosed that Ava would be on the receiving end to her as of yet, knowing she would only fight him if he gave her too much time to process. She worked best under pressure, when she let her instincts shine.

Cassius started the coffee pot as Amora strode down the stairs in a fluffy pink robe.

"You're up early," she cooed.

He did not turn to look at her.

"I have always been an early riser."

She slid her hands around his waist

and he felt the weight of the world. He could not deny that the touch was nice, but it didn't feel *right*.

The hands he wanted to touch him belonged to someone else.

So he moved away, out of Amora's grasp.

"Oh, Cassius, why do you fight this?" she asked as she leaned against the counter.

Cassius opened the cabinets, looking until he'd found a mug.

"Amora..."

"Tell me why, Cassius. Why do you deny the things you were made for?" She motioned around the sparkling kitchen. It was pristine, crisp and reminded him of the Medici estate.

"And what is it do you think I am made for *petite étoile*?" He poured himself a cup of coffee, opening her refrigerator. It was empty.

Amora tutted at him as she opened a cabinet, pulling out a container of sugar and powdered creamer. She set the items before him with grace.

"You were made to be a king, Cassius. To live your days in immortal opulence, wanting for nothing. Not to live in the shadows."

"And is that what you have here, Amora? A Kingdom with no King?"

He took the creamer, sniffing it first, and it smelled chemical. He pushed it away, settling on sugar alone.

"What I have is protection. I am a queen, Cassius. I have armies. Fortresses. I can protect you, if that is what you are worried about..."

Cassius took a sip of his coffee.

"Like you protected Marcellus." The moment the words left his mouth, he regretted them. It was a deep cut, even for him.

Amora crossed her arms, the motion driving her breasts together to produce a rather tempting vision. She stood in the light of the kitchen look like someone from another time.

"I know what you are doing. It will not work. You will not wound me with your words so easily. I have fought for this life fang and nail, and my kingdom is of my own making. Marcellus may have given it to me, but it is I who made the Medici name one to be feared, Cassius."

"Not everyone wants a life in the spotlight, on a pedestal. I may have left because of..."

Eden's voice stopped him from

breathing.

He'd never discussed what had happened with anyone other than Leon, for fear she would make good on her threat and find him.

Amora closed the space between them, her forest green eyes full of hunger.

"Stay with me, Cassius. You can feast all you want on fresh, dried, semi-warm blood, whatever you wish, in the comforts you deserve. I would be good to you, Cassius. I could give you what you desire most."

Cassius stared down at her, searching her eyes for an answer he knew he'd never find.

Because the thing he wanted most was not blood, or sex, or beautiful lies.

She slid her delicate fingers along his

shirt, her pink nails catching on the fabric as his phone lit up with a notification.

*Saved by a Crowley.*

He removed her hand gingerly. "I must go."

"Cassius..." she whined as he left his bitter coffee on the counter, heading for the door.

When he reached the elevators, he was met by a woman with sparkling eyes and jet black hair, and for a moment his blood chilled. Though when Enchantress flashed him a smile, he settled only a fraction.

Eden was not here.

She was only in his head, in his memories.

"Rough night?" Enchantress smirked as she pressed the elevator button.

Cassius slid his hands in his pockets.

"I must admit tonight's festivities have me a bit... anxious," he politely answered. He looked over the woman who'd kidnapped his friend. The hallway was empty except for them.

"You vampires are far too dramatic for my taste. Always brooding over everything like some middle grade emo."

Cassius shirked her words. "Excuse me?"

"What do you have to be nervous about? Think you're going to loose?"

"No. I do not. I only mean that I have not been... social... in many years. Crowds tend to make me nervous."

He knew from his own research, his own intuition Enchantress—Caroline, as Amora had called her—favored loners.

The elevator dinged and he motioned

for her to step in. Just because she was a monster did not negate the manners he'd been raised with.

"That's the beauty of the labyrinth. You'll be so focused on the game, you'll hardly realize the people in the room. At least, that's the intention.

"Have you seen the guest list? Know something I don't, my lovely Enchantress?"

Her blue eyes shimmered with mischief. She shrugged.

"Let's just say... this isn't my first labyrinth... what was your name again? Cassius?"

Cassius stilled at the mention of his name on her tongue.

"You have done this before?" he asked as she hit the button for the first floor.

"It's been awhile, but yes. It is a time honored tradition for my kind."

"The Djinn?"

Enchantress's eyes glowed bright aqua for a moment. "Yes. Many a times we have given man... and creature everything they desire. They only need to prove themselves worthy, and say the magic words, of course."

Enchantress smiled wickedly as the bells sounded on the sixteenth floor.

Cassius's gazr settled on her, the weight of her words hanging in the air between them.

"And what reasons would a Djinn have to be working underneath a vampire like *Ami*?"

Caroline leaned closer to him as the tenth floor dinged, the doors opening and closing of their own accord.

"The same reason the rest of us are drawn to Ami. To take back what is ours."

Cassius swallowed nervously. Something about the way her words sounded, their sharp sting made him feel on edge.

"And what is that?"

"Power, darling. What else?"

"Amora promises you power?"

"Ami promises us the chance to have our cake and finally eat, Cassius. We are hungry, too, but we do not have the means to eat whenever we wish. We can only feed every so many years, and we must make the meal worthwhile."

He watched as the elevator neared the fifth floor.

"I supposed I will see you there, Cassius, was it?"

Cassius nodded his head in approval. "Of course."

# CHAPTER TWENTY-TWO

THE GRAND OPENING of the Marquis Masquerade and Fun House was apparently a larger event than Ava had realized. It seemed as though everywhere she went, the only thing the folks of Albright wanted to talk about was the masquerade bar. The costumer where she'd purchased her dress at the last minute raved about the amount of costumes she'd sold in preparation for the event alone, with a smile, as if it was some sort of accomplishment. Though Ava could hardly see the accomplishment knowing that the individuals arriving at the bar this evening would only be dressed for death. She hoped that perhaps they could stake or kill at least a few of the ticks and Djinn. Perhaps she could try to ritual again, smear some dead Djinn juice on her mark. Clearly, she'd missed a step in her alcohol induced haze the prior night.

Ava sighed as she scrubbed at her scalp, letting the shampoo run in sudsy streams down her back. The hot water was soothing, calming even. After one last Scooby Gang meeting in which her brother and Dallas had discussed in great detail the plan, she did not wait to jump into the shower. It'd been nearly forty eight hours at this point, and while she was certain no one else could notice, she could.

She'd just turned off the faucets, wrapping herself in a pale blue, fluffy towel when Dallas called her name from the doorway.

"Ava." His voice was soft, pulling her from her thoughts as she turned around in the bathroom. Dallas stood against the door, shirtless, his large arms crossed in front of his chest.

"What do you want?" she grumbled as she tightened the towel around her front.

"There's a lot of things I want, Ava, but right now? I just want you to look at me."

Ava fought the desire to meet his eyes, losing miserably.

"Jake..." She sighed tirelessly.

"Just listen to me, Ava. I need to say this. I didn't ask for any of this to happen. You, me. Us. I tried to fight it, I really did, but..."

Ava suddenly felt cold, despite the steam in the room.

"But what?" Her voice was barely a whisper. "There was never supposed to be an us. It was just supposed to be sex, no strings attached... We have a job to do, Dallas." Even as she said the words aloud, she could feel the sting, the pain of them. She'd never said it out loud before.

"I know. But somewhere along the way Ava, in the middle of all the blood and the bullshit... I... I fell in love with you."

He took a step closer, and she did not

stop him. He reached out, brushing her wet hair back behind her shoulder, his thumb tracing over her jaw. Ava felt as if she couldn't speak.

"I can't be what you want me to be, you know that right? I'll never be this—" She waved around the pale, seashell blue bathroom, with its beige towels and perfectly set tile.

"I'll never be this person. I'm defective. I don't run right, I..." Thoughts of waking in a room filled with monsters threatened to pull her under, the words on the edge of her tongue.

Dallas slid his hand around her waist, shifting the towel just above her thighs.

"This is who I was Ava, not who I am. You know me better than anyone."

"Loving me is a death wish, Jake.

Nothing good can come from it..." she whispered.

"I'm not your parents, or Ross," he said, running his fingers down her heated skin. He closed his eyes, leaning his forehead against hers.

"Those fucking ticks took everything from me. Until I found your brother, until I found you..."

Ava slid her hands up around his neck, feeling the edges of his short hair.

"I forgot what it felt like to have something to fight for." The rumble of his deep voice echoed through her entire being as his lips brushed hers. Her tears melted against his skin as he kissed her softly.

It was... new. He'd never kissed her with such sweetness before.

"What it felt like to have *someone*

worth fighting for."

"Oh, Jake..." Ava cried out as she kissed him with trembling lips.

He broke away, leaving her feeing more exposed than she'd ever been before. His fingers brushed the underside of her wrist, dancing along the raised skin where fangs had once claimed her blood.

"And I'll fight to the death for you, if that's what it takes. I promise."

His words were a promise she was certain he couldn't keep, but in that moment, Ava believed him, because no one had ever made such a declaration to her before.

"I'm sorry for the things I said," she choked out.

"I know, Kitten. Me too."

When his lips met hers again, Ava

pulled him close. Dallas backed her against the sink, lifting her with ease. Her towel fell to the ground with a soft thump as he carried her across the hall, the cool air of the house causing her nipples to stiffen, shockwaves of lust ebbing through her body as she brushed them against his heated chest.

Dallas laid her down on cool, upturned sheets, and she did not waste a moment. The sheets welcomed her into their soft prison as desire flooded her from head to toe. She was frustrated, she was angry, she was scared.

Of all the things they were, and all the things she knew they could be.

She removed his shirt, her fingers deftly working at his jeans, sliding them down as her insides started to twist, readying herself for what she knew was to come.

Dallas's cock sprang free as he settled himself on top of her, dragging his thickness along her wet seam.

"I don't want to fight anymore, Jake," she whispered, gazing into his bright blue eyes with a burgeoning desire she'd never felt before.

Hope.

Her thighs clenched as she bucked her hips off the bed, seeking the friction, wanting nothing more than to be fulfilled by the promise of Dallas's cursed words.

She knew they were doomed. From the moment she kissed him in a boxing ring all those years ago.

But death at the hand of Jake Dallas was as close to bliss as she was going to get.

***

Dallas parked the car up the road from the parking lot, which was already starting to look full.

Thanks to Vinny's blueprints, they discovered a cellar storm door in the woods off the property, which Ava had exited from previously. Lights were lit up on the porch of the Masquerade, and the sounds of electronic symphony music abounded in the chilly air.

Ava bunched up her skirt as Dallas opened the door. Like her, he'd opted for a costume if only to blend in among the crowd when the doors opened. She hadn't asked where he'd gotten his Phantom-esque costume, and she suspected by the frayed edges of his collar it was older than the costume she'd been saddled with.

Ava was still unsure of just *what* she was going to do to distract a room full of vampires and Djinn, and she hoped whatever it was would buy them all enough time for Malcolm and Cassius to find Bryan and escape.

The unmistakable sound of Dallas's motorcycle broke the silence, and Ava let her iridescent, eighties-style ball gown down to the ground.

Of all the ensembles in the costume shop, did the only one in her size *have* to be white?

She longed for pants.

The headlight on the motorcycle shined on her like a laser beam, catching the fabric and making the sequins pop to life.

Dallas stood behind her in his costume, which she had to admit didn't look half bad on him, especially with his phantom mask. The way the fabric clung to his muscles—particularly the pants— she couldn't deny he was a sight for sore eyes.

But as Cassius pulled up on Dallas's motorcycle, Ava felt the air leave her lungs.

He still wore his signature leather pants, but he'd traded his normal heathered shirts in for a ruffled blouse, the kind that exposed a sliver of his pale chest just enough. Combined with his golden hair and glowing green eyes, he looked like something out of a fantastical dream, like a Goblin King come to whisk her away to a world of floating stairs.

"You clean up nice," she teased him. "A little on the nose, though, if you ask me."

"Says the woman who looks like a frosted cupcake," he said smoothly.

"Where's your mask?" she asked, feeling strangely on the spot.

Cassius pulled out the black venetian mask, sliding it over his head.

"And yours?" he breathed, his voice full of darkness.

Ava took in the sight of him, standing before her and she could not deny the way her blood responded. Her body heated at the sight, but she was certain it had to do with the prospect of slaying and nothing else.

"I've never been one to follow the rules." She smirked.

Dallas shook his head.

"I am certain you don't need one, what with your blinding frock and all," he teased her. "Are you ready to save the day, Ava?" Cassius offered her his arm. She contemplated taking it. Setting her hand on his forearm, letting him lead her into a den full of monsters hungry for blood.

Her scar burned in his presence, as if it knew her blood truly belonged to him.

So instead of giving in to the instinct, she pushed past Cassius and headed for the Marquis.

# CHAPTER TWENTY-THREE

CASSIUS LOOKED JAKE Dallas in the eye as he sauntered past him, after Ava.

"I trust you will find that I have taken good care of her," he said smoothly, his lips curling back to expose just a hint of fang.

Dallas's eyes narrowed, his breathing steady.

"Well, I would hope so. After all, she wasn't yours to begin with," he said gruffly.

"I even polished the chrome." Cassius slid his hands in his pockets.

Dallas grunted as he set toward his motorcycle, swinging his leg over it.

"You fuck this up for us and I will kill you. And I won't be sorry about it."

Cassius picked up his pace as Dallas started up the shimmering, silver bike, taking off toward the Marquis.

They'd been over the plans enough. While Malcolm was inside, biding his time until the labyrinth would start, Dallas was to stake out their exit, ready to receive them all once he and Malcolm had obtained their target and completed the rescue.

He knew from Amora's admission that the conspiracy-theorizing coroner was being kept in the suit closest to the labyrinth's underground entrance, if only for convenience.

Cassius hoped at the very least Bryan had been treated well in captivity. When it came to servitude, Amora did have a history of being quite... demanding. But she could also be quite amenable and manipulative.

Eden preferred to kill to have her way, whereas Amora preferred a much slower, painful sort of torment to get what she wanted out of her subjects.

He'd seen such things firsthand. Given the fact the Djinn had been feeding the spots their deepest desires, he wondered how strong Bryan would be.

Would he falter?

Or would he persist to escape?

Ava tromped through the grass on the

side of the road, and he could see that underneath her poofy, shimmering skirt and tulle, she was wearing her signature black studded boots. The sight made him smile. Underneath it all, there was no hiding the real Ava Crowley. Though he had to admit, she was quite stunning in her shimmering ball gown. The sweetheart neckline showed off her ample cleavage, the sash that fell off her shoulders exposing her slender, pale neck.

Cassius's throat constricted, the sight a most favorable one to him. He could feel her pulse in his veins, steady like a river. He hoped the blood bags he'd stolen from the hospital morgue on his way would suffice enough to get him through the masquerade. Dallas was not the only one worried that things would go awry.

Cassius hated large events such as this, for many reasons. But for his friends he'd always proven loyal to a fault.

*Penny, Marguerite, Marcellus.*

*Leon.*

*Eden.*

Her words reverberated in his head, the sting of them still fresh even though the'd been uttered ages ago.

*"Do what you do best, Cassius."*

*"What is that?" he asked.*

*"Be the hero," Eden whispered.*

Though as Cassius looked at the fresh-faced slayer, her stark profile and her ruby red lips, staring at the Marquis with determination, he knew he was far from a hero.

At least where Ava Crowley was

concerned.

"How many stakes are you hiding in there?" he teased her.

Ava huffed as they came to the parking lot.

"Bold of you to assume all I am hiding is stakes. A girl likes to accessorize, you know."

"And what sort of accessories do you favor, my sweet Avarice?"

"Sharp, pointy, sparkly things, of course. And matches, naturally."

"Plan on starting a fire this evening?"

"We all have our vices, Cas," she said as they approached the front of the Marquis.

Up close it reminded him of another place, a long time ago.

The Duquensian manor where he'd first danced with Eden. He hadn't known much of the world he'd been born into at the time, and he was so fresh, so new. He'd only just completed his transition, and the thirst was maddening. When a beautiful, raven-haired woman found him in the shadows, feasting on blood with guilt and remorse, he hadn't known what she was truly offering. He'd been far too trusting then, far too naive to the evils of the world around him.

Cassius shoved the thoughts of his past down, back into their coffin where they belonged as he stared up at the lights, feeling strangely anxious.

Ava shifted her stance, the movement bringing her closer to him. It was just an innocent motion, something she probably didn't even notice. Still, he felt a sort of peace in her proximity every time she closed the space between them, every time she absentmindedly fell into the gravitational pull that existed between them, and every time he pretended not to notice.

"If we pull this off… you owe me a donut," she said seriously.

"My sweet Avarice, do not sell yourself short. *When* we pull this off, I will buy you a dozen donuts. And coffee with French vanilla cream, and two sugars."

Ava lifted her skirts as she walked forward, taking the lead.

Cassius was more than happy to let her lead him.

# CHAPTER TWENTY-FOUR

AVA WAS NOT sure what to expect from a funhouse slash masquerade, but she was certain the shadowed, dark, winding hallway was not anywhere in her imagination.

"Amora has always had a thing for theatrics," Cassius mused, and Ava twisted her lips.

"I thought you said this was a party. You know like... full of people?"

"I believe it is the light at the end of this literal tunnel," he said as he motioned to the hallway. Like many haunted houses, it looked as if inflated black bags stemmed from the walls to create a claustrophobic tunnel in which sensory deprivation was the terror experienced.

No light, only darkness.

"The only way out is through," she mused aloud as she lifted her skirts, moving to take one step in front, but Cassius did not let her.

"For a fan of horror movies, are you not missing the most obvious trope? The beautiful woman *never* goes headfirst in the darkness lest she has a death wish," he teased her.

Ava felt the heat in her blood start to boil. She wasn't scared, knowing what lay at the other end of the stupid hallway.

*Monsters.*

*A labyrinth.*

*A friend needing to be rescued.*

*A Djinn who could possibly break the Goblin King beside her's claim on her.*

"With this contraption—"She gestured to her dress. " I'm fairly certain I've got enough of a buffer."

Cassius stepped in front of her, sliding his arm in between the crevice, extending his opposite arm toward her. Offering her his hand, yet again.

Ava looked at it, feeling strangely warm. But she knew time was of the essence, and so she took his hand.

His long, pale fingers curled around hers. His touch was cool, gentle, as his fingers brushed the scar on her wrist with care as if it were fresh.

Her palm heated like a fire, her body temperature rising.

*Surely it is from the overabundance of tulle.*

Cassius tugged her hand with a force that was somehow both strong and soft, as if he was terrified to let her go but frightened all the same.

She watched as the darkness swallowed him, and followed him down the rabbit hole.

In the darkness there was only the two of them, molded together by fire and ice.

And as soon as it was there, it was gone. For the light appeared, but it was not golden or incandescent. It was ultraviolet and neon, and it was reflective.

They'd come to a room of mirrors, bathed in hazy blue and violet, their reflections infinite.

He was everywhere.

All around her, encompassing her like air.

The sound of music echoed around them, and by the sound of it, they were close to the party.

"I guess this will have to make up for the haunted houses I missed this year," she said sarcastically. Though she had no reason to do so, she could not help but tighten her grip on the annoying vampire in front of her. Every bone in her body told her this was a trap. She'd been had. She'd finally lost her mind, and this was it. This was how he would take her, in a fun house, surrounded by mirrors and a thumping base.

Cassius let go of her hand, turning to look at her with deep, glowing green eyes that made her feel a sting of guilt.

Her hand fell to her side and the heat subsided.

When they'd arrived on the other side of the room, the path became much easier.

As they entered the grand ballroom, Ava had to admit it looked like something out of a movie. The room was large, cavernous, and it was difficult to believe it existed within the size of the building she'd laid eyes on.

In the center of the room was what looked like a large enclosure or fish tank, able to be viewed from all sides. Her wrist flared with heat, burning beneath her skin like lava as her skin prickled with goosebumps.

She glanced around, uncertain of who was a vampire and who was not. There were plenty of individuals wearing masks, which only added to the mystery. She knew the Djinn were hiding somewhere in the crowd...

In the years she'd been tracking vamps, she'd rarely come across other monsters. Save for the time she'd spent in Mahoning, in the mountains hunting werewolves, or that time she'd been bitten by an Incubus...

But in all those situations, she'd been able to pick them out with a defining factor. In the presence of an Incubus, her mark felt like ice, and in the presence of the werewolves, she could tell by their glowing gold eyes and physique, not to mention they all looked... similar in appearance.

"What's wrong?" Cassius's voice was soft in her ear. He was right behind her, yet he kept his distance.

"I cannot tell the difference," she whispered. "Between vampire and Djinn."

Cassius let out a breath, his voice low enough only she could hear.

"I don't feel anything in their presence, but they all share a similar... aesthetic."

Ava turned to look at him. "You do realize everyone's wearing masks, right?"

"They all have the same aquamarine eyes, the same complexion and dark hair. Their aura is inviting. It is not dissimilar from a vampire's thrall. It is meant to lure, so it will smell heavenly, make you feel relaxed. But their scent is spicy, citrus-like. Woods like. They smell like the lands they originated from."

"Great. So I'm looking for blue-eyed goths who smell like Morrocan oil. That helps a ton," she spewed.

Ava could feel eyes on her, and she wanted to grab her stake. Instead, she put one foot in front of the other and approached the glass, if only to get a better view.

Cassius followed her, keeping close. He left a modicum of space between them, enough that only she could hear his whispering plea.

"Stay close."

When they'd arrived at the glass, she set her sweaty palm against it. Looking down into the glass, she could see the hedges and walls set up, and she could see the spots waiting at various corners.

"My money's on that one," a man said

as he came next to her. His olive skin was sickly in the artificial light that emanated from the labyrinth.

"The skinny one?" she asked.

The man with grey eyes pointed to a spot on the other side of where he stood.

"Yeah, that one. Ami got a last minute spot. Heard he took out a guard on the way into the labyrinth when they was loading 'em up. Scrappy one, he is."

"Where is *Ami?*" Cassius asked smoothly.

"Probably downstairs fussing over the details. Woman and their parties," the man scoffed.

Ava's heart stopped as she ventured around the man, looking through the glass to see he was pointing at a man dressed in ripped jeans and a Led Zeppelin shirt.

Her brother. Of course he'd stick out like a sore thumb.

*You're supposed to blend in, Mal.*

"And who are you placing your bets on?" the man asked curiously, but Ava was certain he was not talking to her.

"Wise choice, my friend. That spot belongs to me."

The words on Cassius's tongue angered Ava. It sounded wrong coming out Cassius's mouth, but yet...

He was a monster just like the rest of him, and she had to remember that.

She had to remember who he was, and who she was.

For once she got her hands on the blood of a Djinn—perhaps she could find Enchantress—she would be free of his bond, forever.

"Does this lovely delicate flower

belong to you as well?" the man asked smoothly.

Ava's stomach felt nauseous. She belonged to no one, but how could a monster understand such things.

"She is free to answer you herself. She has a voice."

Cassius looked to her for only a second, exposing a hint of fang. He regarded her with a sly look.

Ava's fingers ached to drive a stake through *something*, and this man's words caused her fire to spark. She could not very well walk into a rich vault and not leave with a small fortune. Perhaps she'd found the distraction they all needed.

"I belong to no one," she said boldly.

"What a pity," he said as he offered her his hand. "But perhaps in that case,

I can persuade you for a dance?" The man smiled.

"I'd love to," she mused sweetly, if only to seem appreciative. Ava could feel the beginnings of a thrall reaching out to latch on to her with desperation.

*Of course, Cassius had said Djinn were capable of similar things...*

She tried to get a good look at the man's eyes, but it was hard to discern amidst his brown leather bird mask.

But Ava would not so easily give in. She'd been here a hundred times. In the arms of a vampire, fighting their jedi mind tricks. Djinn or not, she had faith she could take this monster either way.

And so, she pretended to fall into the arms of the unknown man, channeling her inner Christine. Ava let him pull her to the center of the ballroom floor, and she could feel Cassius's gaze on her like a sun burning down on the sidewalk in July.

She stared up at the man, his facial features strangely familiar to her, though she couldn't place them. His eyes were the shade of oceans.

"Do I... know you?" she asked.

He slid his hands around her waist, turning her around so her ass was smack against his groin. A deep rumble left his chest, and she could feel the faint stirrings of lust in her belly as his thrall-aura-whatever jedi mind tricks he was using, seeped out toward her like an invisible Kraken ready to sink a ship.

Ava called on the memories like they were weapons themselves. And in a away, they were.

*The moan of pleasure before Ross's*

*scream.*

*Her parents cold, dead eyes staring back at her across a bloodstained carpet.*

*Sam Kingsley floundering around on the floor of a burning building as she exorcised him.*

*Watching Dallas disappear with Midnight at the Drowned Clam.*

"I am hurt, my dear. I would have thought you'd remembered our time together, however brief it was." His left hand pulled along her waist, sliding down her thigh. His right grasped her wrist.

Ava stilled as he dragged his fangs along her neck torturously and it all came rushing back.

The drinks, the dancing. His hands around her waist, pulling her closer. His eyes as he took in the sight of her before him, his teeth along the scars of her thigh, his blood smeared in her open wound, his hand wrapped around his cock as he stroked himself until he'd brought himself to release with a groan, while Ava felt *free*.

*Hopeful.*

*Wishing for release of her own.*

The nameless man from the bar. Her insides twisted with nausea once more, but her face did not betray her sudden remembrance.

"How could I forget... silly me." She shoved down the panic, the disgust and the regret, bending over to grind her ass against him as she bunched her skirts just enough she could grasp her knife. As she had told Cassius, she'd opted to bring silver with her in case of Djinn. And if she was correct, the silver would turn this man, this creature, to putty, causing him to die a slow and agonizing death. Just enough to buy them some time...

When she whirled around faster than a hurricane, her knife striking his chest, he growled ferociously.

"You little bitch!" He grunted as she pulled the knife out. She watched the blood pool against his white shirt. "She's a slayer!" he yelled, and suddenly Ava felt more in danger than ever before.

As she drove the blade in the nameless man's gut, she could feel the stare of those around her, and hungry growls sounded.

Vampires stared at her with hunger, and at the Djinn who daws now kneeling on the floor, the blood seeping through the spots she'd stabbed him. She'd heard not all supernaturals were as picky when it came to their prey. Though there was the legend or two of vampires who relished in supernatural blood, such as the ones they'd run into in Mahoning, but they'd killed those vampires...

"Ava, run!" Cassius hollered, just as the man roared an animalistic, angry sound. The sound was answered, echoing in the dark space like a war cry. The scent of blood was pungent in the air.

His blood smelled rotten and awful and she wanted to throw up. She did not have time to strike a match as the crowd closed around her. She did not have time to process or steal the blood as she wished, to see if it would fix her cursed mark.

If it would cure her.

Ava looked Cassius in the eye, seeing the fear shine in his gorgeous irises, spreading like wildfire. He was scared, too. His gaze darted to the puddle of blood forming beneath the man.

She did not think twice about running.

This was it, this was the moment they'd been waiting for. She ran toward the other end of the room, remembering Vinny's blueprints in her head. She hoped the gamble she'd taken was worth it.

Vampires hissed, Djinn snarling behind her as they fought one another for the body on the ground.

Cassius grabbed her hand as she ran to him. His grip was firm, strong.

"I said a distraction, Ava, not a free

for all," he said as he pulled her toward the other end of the room. A creature with dark hair and fangs lunged for them, but Cassius easily dodged her.

Ava could barely keep up with his pace, but she didn't care. The scent of woodsy citrus perfumed the air as she started to feel hazy. She focused on the looming exit sign and the door beneath it that led to the basement below, and she followed it like a guiding star.

# CHAPTER TWENTY-FIVE

"WHERE DO YOU think you're going?" A deep voice sounded as Cassius and Ava came to the door.

He held Ava's wrist tightly, squeezing, if only to tell her without words to follow his lead. He prayed she would not open her mouth, or try anything.

"Taking this one down to the cells where she belongs, of course. Thought she could get one up on us."

The guard appraised them both, and Cassius did not miss the way he looked over Ava.

"All that caused by this little thing?" The guard set his hand on his hip, and Cassius could feel thrall in the air.

Instinctively, he pushed back against it, causing the man to look at him with curiosity.

"I can take her from here."

"That won't be necessary," Cassius said solidly.

Ava faltered in his grasp, and he could see her eyelashes fluttering.

Cassius moved toward the guard, bearing his fangs. He forced Ava behind him.

"Get downstairs to the labyrinth, Ava."

'Cas...' She sounded as if she wanted

to protest, but thought better of it.

"When I say now..." he spoke evenly as the guard bared his own fangs, drawing his own weapon.

A gun.

Cassius did not think twice as he lunged for the guard, dropping Ava's hand.

"Now!" he hollered, as hands and bodies collided.

Out of the corner of his eye he could see her glittering sequins, glinting like pixies in the sunlight, and within seconds the slam of the door told him she was gone.

Well on her way to the labyrinth.

The guard pushed back against him, and they danced a waltz of hissing, of bared fangs. The guard grabbed him, pulling him against his chest, the barrel pointed to his jugular.

"Give me one good reason I shouldn't blow your fucking brains out," he hissed.

"Amal, that is enough!" A sweet, saccharine voice called, and the guard stilled. His hand shook, but he did not remove his gun.

Out of the shadows, Amora emerged.

"Oh, Cassius, you haven't changed at all, have you?"

Cassius laid his eyes on her, and she looked positively regal, dressed in a long, blush colored silk dress. The high slit at the thigh made her naturally petite frame look longer, taller even. Her pale golden hair cascaded down her shoulders, her blood red lips pressed into a thin line.

And she was not alone.

The well dressed Djinn woman

behind her smirked devilishly as her icy eyes appraised him.

"What is her name this time? Helen? Rose? Jennifer?" Amora shook her head.

Cassius bit his tongue as he looked away.

"It is not what it looks like," he said.

Enchantress took one step closer to him.

"He is no different than the rest of them, Ami. He lies to you."

Amora pouted before sighing. "Amal, lower your weapon."

The guard broke out into a sweat, shakily obeying.

"I wish I could say I was surprised, Cassius. I really do. But it seems you have crossed me for the last time. Fool me once, shame on you. Fool me twice, well..."

Enchantress stepped forth and the air burst with woody, citrusy perfume, and Cassius started to feel hazy, relaxed. As if heaven was so close, but somehow so far away...

"Amora... petite étoile," he called.

Amora sighed. "Do what you wish, Caroline. I have no need for traitors," Amora said as she turned on her heel.

At that very moment, Amal fell to the ground, his gun skittering to the floor.

"Please, don't hurt me, I'm sorry, I—"

Cassius watched in shock and awe as the guard looked to be seeing something that wasn't there. A hallucination of sorts, but whatever it was he was seeing, it was obviously distressing.

"Oh, I'm going to enjoy this," she said as she reached out, grasping a hold of Cassius.

He felt immobile, as if he was not in control. He fought to try and move, but it was useless. Panic coursed through him as he worried perhaps it was not Enchantress or Amora who controlled him.

Perhaps his worst nightmare had made itself known again... after all these years...

Enchantress grabbed him by the throat.

"Any last requests?" she purred just as she sunk her claws into his skin, her fangs into his neck.

Cassius could feel his blood rushing to the surface, but he felt strangely at peace.

"Such desperation, such pain. You are ripe with hope, aren't you?"

Cassius struggled to move his arms,

to fight the Djinn off.

Her eyes glowed bright like bioluminescent algae on the surface of a lake.

The world around him started to fade, disappearing into something else. His blood slowed, his heart rate stilling.

The world was so... beautiful he had to close his eyes.

When he opened them, he was right back where he'd started. In the ballroom, holding Ava's hand as she ignored the man talking about the spots.

"Perhaps I could ask for a dance?" he spoke softly as he tugged her closer. Ava looked up at him with curiosity, a blush creeping onto her cheeks.

"You can always ask," she teased him.

"But will you ever say yes?" He pulled

her closer, settling his right hand around her waist.

Ava smirked, shaking her head as she set her hand in his open left palm.

"Yes," she spoke the words softly. The swooning melancholic melodies of a song he'd heard long ago echoed in the room, the words filling him with faith in every step.

The music ebbed and flowed as the people around them waltzed and wallowed, hiding behind their grotesque and stunning masks. The scent of blood in the air was thick.

Ava leaned her head to the side, showcasing the expanse of her slender, pale neck.

"Is this what you want, Cassius?" she asked.

His thirst was insatiable.

"Yes," he whispered. The world was spinning and his heart felt as if it could leap right out of his chest.

Ava slid her arms around his neck, pulling him to her. Her fingers grasped the edges of his hair at the nape of his neck. Chest to chest, he could feel her heartbeat, her stolen pulse in his veins.

"Is this what you wish for?" she asked.

Cassius felt the overwhelming need to say yes, but something stopped him. It sounded like someone was calling his name.

Her voice...

"Cassius! Run!" Ava hollered.

Ava...

*But she is right here...*

A wet, crunching sound followed by a hiss filtered through his thoughts, and he blinked. The world started to dissipate again, the wondrous moments gone with the wind.

Enchantress fought against Ava, baring her fangs, her face contorted in the grotesque true form of the Djinn.

Ava kicked at her, knocking her on her back as she drove her knife through Enchantress's pale, exposed chest.

The Djinn writhed beneath her, underneath the torn and shredded edges of Ava's white ball gown, which was covered in debris and blood. Burgundy stains spattered along the iridescent fabric, along her pale arms. Blood oozed from her wrists, where he'd lain claim to her blood.

His neck throbbed, and he brought his hand to the spot. When he pulled away he could see blood. Thick, black blood covered his hands. He'd been bitten.

Ava rose from the Djinn who lay lifeless on the floor, waving her hand in front of his face." He blinked once more, focusing on her.

"Get Bryan out of here," she commanded. He blinked once again, realizing he was on the floor beneath the exit. The way out was not too far, but he was aware of the fighting going on still, and the sounds of sirens outside.

How long had he been out?

When his gaze landed on his friend, it all came crawling back. Bryan's tired, heavy eyes and sullen appearance was both disheartening and full of relief.

He was alive.

He was alive, and now he was safe, as long as they could get out of this hellhole in one piece.

"Go, get out of here! Get Bryan back to the car and—"

"I am not leaving without you," Cassius said as he got up. Bryan stood beside him, covered in sweat and blood, and Cassius hoped it wasn't his. The scent caused his stomach to turn, his throat to dry and he had to fight it.

A wretched scream tore through the air, and Ava's eyes widened in fear.

"Just go! Fucking listen to me!"

She shoved at them, and Cassius felt between a rock and a hard place. He wrapped his arm around Bryan, trusting his gut.

"We will wait for you," he said, hoping she understood.

Ava nodded as another scream echoed in the air, and she wasted no time disappearing into the darkness below, leaving Cassius and Bryan to fend for themselves.

# CHAPTER TWENTY-SIX

THE SOUND OF Dallas's scream made Ava's blood curl. She raced down the stairs, practically leaping all the way down.

When she finally got down to where she'd left her brother and Dallas, her heart stopped.

They were fighting off a handful of monsters.

Ava's wrist flared with heat and

prickled with goosebumps, and she wasted no time defending her brother and Dallas. The world moved in slow motion, as she, Dallas, and Malcolm moved in perfect symmetry, a symphony of knives and stakes.

When she was certain they'd cleared out the herd, she let her hand fall, her gaze falling on a bloodied Malcolm, whose shirt was in shreds.

"We did it," she said as she caught her breath.

Malcolm pulled her into his arms.

"We fucking did it," he said with a laugh.

Ava had never felt so accomplished.

And then she smelled the scent of burning wood and citrus.

"Ava, look out!" Dallas's voice cut through as he shoved her and Malcolm aside.

The sound of fangs sinking in through flesh and muscle echoed in the air as Ava turned around, expecting to see Dallas strong-arming whatever monster had decided to show up late to the party.

But that was not the sight that greeted Ava.

"Dallas!" she hollered as the Djinn clutched a writing Dallas to its chest. Blood seeped out of his neck and he cried out in pain.

Ava and her brother lunged for him, fighting to pull the Djinn off. Malcolm sunk his blade in its back, the creature hissing in pain.

It let go, Dallas falling limp to the ground, and Ava scrambled to him. His eyes looked scared as he looked around.

Her hand settled over his neck, trying to stop the bleeding. But it just kept coming.

"Come on, Jake, you gotta get up. We gotta get out of here," she exclaimed, her voice shaking.

"I'm sorry, Kitten, but that's not happening."

"Jake..." Malcolm rushed to his side, flanking Ava.

"You guys need to get out of here." His voice sounded garbled, like he couldn't breathe.

Ava felt sticky, warm blood seeping all through her dress, and as she moved away a hair, she saw he was bleeding from the chest. A long, gaping gash in his side oozed blood. She could see the faint coloring of bone.

"Rule number one," Ava said as tears

came to her eyes. "No one gets left behind," she sobbed.

Dallas reached out, brushing away a strand of her hair.

His touch was cold.

Because he was dying.

She knew it in her heart, but she couldn't process it. For this was Jake Dallas. He was a lot of things, but he was not so easily bested.

She'd seen him take down much stronger monsters, and she'd heard the stories. The man practically had nine lives from all the hunter tales she'd heard.

Malcolm's arms wrapped around her.

"You have a job to do." He coughed.

"*We* have a job to do," she pleaded.

Dallas shook his head, looking up at Malcolm.

"I can see her," he said wistfully.

Malcolm's sobs echoed with her own as he spoke.

"She's waiting for you. They both are." Malcolm pulled Dallas to him, and then that was it. The sound of his knife driving deep into his blood soaked body was the last thing Ava heard.

She let out a bloodcurdling scream as she felt Dallas's cold hand fall from hers. The world was blurry as Malcolm wrapped her in his embrace, as he pulled her by the hand through the dark cavernous hallways, through the basement of the Marquis.

***

When they'd made it to the clearing, she could see Cassius leaning against the hood of her Impala, could see Bryan's defeated eyes gazing out at them through her windows.

"You are all right, you..." His voice faded. "Where is Dallas?" he asked, his voice a whisper.

Malcolm only shook his head. Ava could not speak, the words stuck in her throat, making it hard to breathe.

*Dead.*

Dallas was dead.

# CHAPTER TWENTY-SEVEN

THE DRIVE HOME was much quicker in time, but it felt like an eternity.

The news of the murders at the Marquis Masquerade had made the radio stations and the papers by morning. According to the news outlets, they'd come across six bodies, and Cassius could not help but feel a sense of guilt. Ava could have been one of them, but she wasn't.

Was it wrong to feel a sense of relief that the slayer had survived when her lover did not?

Cassius felt conflicted on the matter. He was glad they'd accomplished their mission, they'd rescued their friend, who was sleeping soundly, snoring like a grizzly bear in his own bed. Cassius shut the door, vowing to stop by in the morning to make sure his friend was alright after all he'd been through.

Ava leaned against the drivers side door, standing as still as a statue.

*At least she's moved since we left Ohio...*

Cassius came to her side, his heart aching. Her stolen pulse throbbed in his veins, slow and steady. The light in her eyes had darkened.

"Ava—"

"Don't." She spoke concisely, curtly. "Don't you fucking—" Her voice shook, as she pinched the bridge of her nose. "Just... listen to me for once and leave me the fuck alone," she cried.

Cassius reached his thumb out, resting it on her cheek.

She grabbed him by the wrist, her nails digging into his skin.

# CHAPTER TWENTY-EIGHT

A SINGLE TEAR melted into her skin as he brushed it away. Ava threw his hand down.

"Get the fuck away from me," she growled.

A part of her wanted to fight. To lay a stake in his chest and blame him for what had happened. Had they not embarked on this journey to find Bryan, perhaps Dallas would still be alive, texting her in the middle of the night, and she would ignore him out of annoyance while secretly dreaming of the next hunt, the next time they'd see one another.

The next fight, the next kiss.

The next case.

But there would be no next anything's.

Not anymore.

The other part of her longed to fall into the vampire in front of her and disappear.

Cassius let out a sigh as he took a step back, his gorgeous green eyes imploring hers as he spoke breathlessly, in defeat.

"As you wish, my sweet Avarice."

And with that he was gone, faded into the shadows of night and Ava was alone once more.

She double checked Bryan's doors were locked, walked the perimeter of his humble abode merely four times before she felt as if she could leave. She wiped her tears away as she started the car, turning the radio up.

The familiar sounds of *Don't Fear The Reaper* played through her speakers, but even that could not soothe her broken heart or her fractured soul.

# EPILOGUE

*Four Days Later*

"JAKE DALLAS WAS my best friend. My partner. He was a hell of a lead singer, a pain in my ass, and a fucking gem," Mal said as he stared into the fire.

To the rest of the world, Dallas had simply died in the brawl at the Marquis. Malcolm had stayed behind to make arrangements, retrieving his body, burning it. Scattering the ashes as Dallas would have wanted.

Malcolm had told them all his wishes were granted, his ashes scattered over the graves of his wife and their unborn child.

*Laura and Kelly Dallas.*

The hits just kept coming, Ava thought.

Would they ever stop?

Would the pain ever subside?

Malcolm set his beer down, and Ava could see he was making his way over to her. He'd asked several times if she wanted to talk, but clearly he did not understand. No amount of talking would fix how she felt, it would not bring him back.

She simply had to cauterize the wound left by Jake Dallas if she wanted to have a semblance of a normal life again.

Whatever normal was for a cursed Crowley.

"How you holding up?" Mal asked, swishing the liquid around in his beer bottle.

"I'm alive, so I guess that counts for something," she said with a scowl. She clutched the maroon hoodie around her waist. The only piece of Jake Dallas she had left.

"You know, this... this is what I was trying to protect you from. This life... it's not for the faint of heart. It's lonely, full of losses. Gruesome, fucked up shit. I wanted to spare you, but... D... he saw something in you, just like he saw something in me."

The bonfire crackled behind them.

Though the courtyard slash backyard of the estate was rather large, Ava couldn't help but feel claustrophobic.

"I don't know if I can do this anymore," she said, her voice filled with defeat.

"It's not us we do this for. It's them," Malcolm said as he nodded to Vinny, Tito, and Hunter all sitting around the fire, beers in hand, telling stories of their friend, their fallen comrade.

"For the ones we've lost. We keep fighting for *them*." Mal let out a shaky breath. "You aren't the only one who loved him, you know. He was my brother, and I can promise you, I will keep fighting for him because I know it's what he would have wanted. And I know he'd want you to do the same."

Ava could not listen to her brother, or

to the stories of Dallas being passed around. Not when she could not speak of her own stories, not when she couldn't speak his name out loud without breaking into tears. Though she wished she could share her memories, be a part of the camaraderie.

To tell of how they'd shared a bucket of wings that first night after Ross's funeral, playing darts, or when he'd gotten all pissed off at her at TerrorCon and kissed her.

The way he hogged the covers in the morning, or the way he held her when she'd been pushed too far.

Perhaps Jake Dallas was not the only one who'd failed miserably.

And now he was gone.

The monsters had taken him, too, just as they had taken Ross, her parents, his wife and child, and once again Ava was alone. Left to bear her heartbreak in silence, her pain, on her own.

"I think I need some air," she said as she rose from her seat, taking her leave. She walked through the house, her footsteps echoing in the space. Malcolm had politely asked Connie to take the day off, if only so they could talk freely about their hunter lives, not having to worry about anyone misunderstanding or asking too many questions.

She settled down on the bench on her porch. The wind kicked up dead leaves, and she sat there for what felt like eternity until a pair of black and white converses peeking out from beneath leather pants came into view.

Ava looked up to see Cassius

standing there, looking as gorgeous as ever, holding out a steaming cup of coffee and a box of donuts.

"What the fuck are you doing here?" she bit.

"I came to express my deepest sympathies," he said softly.

"For a hunter?" she said defensively.

"For a man," he said as he nudged the coffee cup in her direction. "A man who was important to many. Including you."

"Is there whiskey in that?" she asked coldly.

Cassius set the box of donuts down on the patio table, popping the lid open. Ava could see a full box of a dozen donuts, and her stomach lurched for the sugary goodness. She hadn't eaten much in the past few days.

"Only one way to find out," Cassis said with a soft smile.

Ava pulled the coffee cup from his hands, her fingertips brushing his. The touch sent tiny shockwaves through her system that made her feel almost a spark of peace and she pretended not to notice.

"Do you want to talk about what happened?" he asked quietly.

"No."

"May I?" He gestured to the open space beside her.

Ava shrugged. "I don't fucking care."

Cassius sat next to her, leaving nearly a canyon between them.

"Then we will not talk," he said simply.

Ava glanced at the long expanse of his legs in his signature leather pants before sipping the coffee he'd proffered to her.

The unmistakable burn of whiskey in her throat made her eyebrows raise.

"There *is* whiskey in this!"

Cassius shot her a smirk. "A smart woman once told me that coffee fixes most things, and for the rest of life's ills, there is always whiskey."

Ava breathed in the sweet, coffee and cream scent, with a hint of cinnamon, stifling a hint of a smile as he threw her own words back at her.

"I'm too tired to kill you today," she said as she wrapped her fingers around the cup, letting it warm her skin and body. She was tired, near exhausted, and it did help but she would not divulge such things to the vampire beside her.

Cassius crossed his ankles, leaning

back against the bench, leaving a modicum of space between them.

"Perhaps tomorrow then."

Ava took another pull of her strong, alcoholic coffee.

"Tomorrow," she agreed.

They both sat there in silence as the leaves bristled about like tumbleweeds until Ava's insides felt warm, and she'd found enough courage to face the hunters once more. When they'd gone, it was just her and Malcolm.

"I'm leaving tomorrow," he said plainly.

"I'm not surprised. Didn't think you'd stay in one place long."

"I'll be back soon, I just... I have some leads to follow up on. I'll be in touch and I promise I'll be home for Christmas," he said as he pulled some keys out of his pocket. He held them in his hand for a moment before handing them to her.

"What's this?"

"I think he'd want you to have it. The bike."

Ava's chest tightened.

"I can't take that," she said softly.

"Then leave it in the garage with Dad's." Malcolm's voice was quiet.

"I miss him. Dad. He always knew the right thing to say, didn't he?" she said as she wrapped her fingers around the keys tightly.

"Yeah, he did." Mal sighed.

"We're going to avenge them, you know. Mom, Dad, Dallas..." Malcolm pulled her into his arms, and she couldn't help but hug him back.

"I know," she whispered.

"After all, we're fucking Crowley's. It's

in our blood," he said as he broke apart from her.

Ava nodded in response.

"What was that saying Dad always used to say? About fires and rising?"

Mal smiled.

"Ah. I believe it was Carl Sagan's quote, 'stars are phoenixes rising from their own ashes.'"

Ava nodded. "Yup, that's the one."

"Tonight we burn, Ava. But tomorrow, we rise. I promise." He leaned in and kissed her on the cheek.

"Call me when you get in," she said, suddenly feeling exhausted.

"Of course, Simba," Mal said as he headed for the door.

Ava watched from the porch as he drove off, chasing leads, and doing what he did best.

Hunting.

And as she watched him leave, she made a promise to herself to do what she'd been training for for years.

Like a phoenix, she would rise from the ashes of her own destruction and she would fight.


Ava & Cas will fight another day.
In The Blood is AVAILABLE NOW!
http://books2read.com/Forevermore2


Turn the page for a preview of Blood of the Lost...

# PREVIEW

THE AIR WAS thick with broken promises, tainted memories, and the scent of blood. The sound of Ava's screams would haunt Dallas for the rest of his undead life.

Because as Dallas lay motionless on the blood-soaked ground of the Marquis, suspended in motion between life and death, he could feel his insides hardening, changing.

Like a moth inside a cocoon, all he could do was wait. For the transition to take hold.

"Get up," the sound of a woman's voice called to him, but he did not recognize it.

Dallas tried to move his fingers, his toes, but everything felt heavy.

He grunted in response as his eyelashes fluttered. The room he was in was dark, the only light the bright flash from a phone screen.

"Fucking shut that off," he growled, stretching his fingers. He moved his hand to shield his eyes. The light was so bright, blinding almost.

"Oh, this one's got spunk," another woman's voice carried excitedly.

"Who do you think is responsible for making him?"

Dallas attempted to move his legs, the effort nearly exhausting.

His entire body felt as if he'd been hit by a freight train. He held his hand in front of his eyes, noting the mess of blood all over his skin.

Memories filtered back into his brain.

*The Djinn heading for Ava and Mal.*

*How he'd pushed them out of the way, without a second thought.*

There had been so much blood...

Dallas ran his hands over his chest, feeling for the gaping wound he knew should be there.

But he felt no such thing, just cold, congealed blood, and soft, sore skin among the shredded remains of his costume.

"Can you get up?"

Dallas's gaze settled on one of the

women, the one with with the excited voice.

She kneeled before him, long raven waves falling over her shoulders. Her pale skin and glowing aquamarine eyes were indicative of her breed of monster.

*Djinn.*

She looked strangely familiar...

*Dallas leaned in close to the djinn, letting her scent fill his airways. She smelled of woods and citrus and he could feel her natural siren aura trying to capture him.*

*"You got a name, sweetheart, or should I just call you mine?" he asked, the words empty, soulless. It wasn't anything he hadn't done before, but this time... it felt different.*

*Because there was only one woman he wanted to call his, and he'd left her with the vampire who'd claimed her blood...*

*The djinn giggled.*

*Fucking giggled like an innocent child.*

*"You can call me—"*

"Midnight?" Her name came to him without warning as the memories flooded him.

"Oh! You're the guy from the bar... the...hunter..." she said as her eyes widened in surprise.

"He's a hunter?" the other woman shrieked, and Dallas's gaze was pulled away. The other djinn reselmbled Midnight, though she was taller with short chin length black hair that boasted bright blue streaks.

"Ami will have a field day with him..."

Midnight pursed her lips as she set her hand on his shoulder, imploring him with her gaze.

"Perhaps he could be of use to us... to Ami," Midnight said as she tugged Dallas's sleeve.

"Can you get up?" she asked again, her voice soft.

Dallas wiggled his toes in his boots, bending his legs and knees slowly. They still ached, but feeling had come back. He motioned forward, getting up too fast as he started to feel dizzy.

"I'm fine..." he bit, shaking off the touch of the sweet-voiced Djinn.

He could hear the sounds of sirens in the distance, and he knew they were right. He did need to move.

He needed to find Malcolm, Ava...

The thought of the Crowleys caused an ache in his heart as his stomach twisted in nauseous knots.

He was starving. He grabbed his stomach, a painful growl escaping his throat.

"What the fuck..."

"He needs to eat," Midnight protested.

"The damn police will be here any minute, Midnight!" the other one bit out.

Dallas jumped as Midnight slid her hand in his, tugging him toward her.

"Whoever made him doesn't look like they're coming back. He's one of us now. I won't leave him to the fucking wolves."

Dallas tried to make sense of her words, but he couldn't. His head was pounding, his body aching, and he was *starving*. His gaze fell on the short vixen in front of him, his mouth going dry.

*I wish...*

The sound of doors opening, of rushed footsteps, told them all they needed to know.

And so, Jake Dallas followed the djinn into the shadows, escaping into the night.

Watch for Blood of the Lost at your favorite retailer!

# OTHER BOOKS BY ARIEL DAWN

**The Hunter Games**

Blood Of My Enemy

Blood Of The Lost

Thorne Of Blood

**Speed Dating with the Denizens of the Underworld Series**

Hecate

Hades

Orion

Athena

Spike

**The Forevermore Series**

In The Cards

In The Blood

In The Shadows

BLOOD & ASH

In The Deep

In The Garden

In The Night-coming soon!

**Shifters Of Starfall Creek Series**

Hollow's Sunrise

Hollow's Sunset

Hollow's Legacy

Shifters of Starfall Creek Collection:

Books 1-3

Get a copy of Ariel Dawn's short story, Faded, when you sign up for her newsletter!
https://mailchi.mp/e5f326e433bf/dawn-breaks-official-newsletter

# CONNECT WITH ARIEL DAWN

Website

http://www.ariel-dawn.com/

Goodreads:

http://www.goodreads.com/authorariel
dawn

Bookbub:

http://www.bookbub.com/authors/ariel
-dawn

Facebook:

http://www.facebook.com/authorarielda
wn

Twitter:

https://twitter.com/ArielDawn10

Join Dusk Chasers—Ariel Dawn's Official Readers Group for access to exclusive content!

# ABOUT ARIEL DAWN

USA TODAY BESTSELLING AUTHOR Ariel Dawn grew up as an avid reader and is a creative soul.

What started out as writing reviews for indie romance authors led to featuring quirky, stereotypical, and weird covers on her Instagram Wrong Turn Romance, which gave her the courage to finally decide to live her dream and become an author.

Ariel writes plot driven paranormal romance and hopes to venture into fantasy and rom-com in the future. When she isn't writing, she can be found cosplaying, attending conventions, creating all sorts of artwork in her studio, or editing photos for her photography business.

A self-professed geek and foodie, she loves hanging out with family and friends and playing video games and board games with her retro gamer husband.

www.ingramcontent.com/pod-product-compliance
Lightning Source LLC
Chambersburg PA
CBHW061050210726
48294CB00001B/83